Joseph Addison

The Drummer

Or, the Haunted House. A Comedy

Joseph Addison

The Drummer
Or, the Haunted House. A Comedy

ISBN/EAN: 9783337102487

Printed in Europe, USA, Canada, Australia, Japan

Cover: Foto ©Andreas Hilbeck / pixelio.de

More available books at **www.hansebooks.com**

THE
DRUMMER;

OR, THE

HAUNTED HOUSE.

A

COMEDY.

By the late Right Honourable

JOSEPH ADDISON, Esq;

——Falsis terroribus implet
Ut Magus——   Hor.

LONDON,

Printed for M. Dodsley in Pall-mall, and D.
Cooper in the Strand. M DCC LXV.

THE

PREFACE.

HAVING recommended this play to the town, and delivered the copy of it to the bookseller, I think myself obliged to give some account of it.

It had been some years in the hands of the author, and falling under my perusal, I thought so well of it, that I persuaded him to make some additions and alterations to it, and let it appear upon the stage. I own I was very highly pleased with it, and liked it the better, for the want of those studied similes and repartees which we who have writ before him have thrown into our plays, to indulge and gain upon a false taste that has prevailed for many years in the British Theatre. I believe the author would have condescended to fall into this way a little more than he has, had he before the writing of it been often present at theatrical representations. I was confirmed in my thoughts of the play, by the opinion of better judges to whom it was communicated, who observed

that

that the fcenes were drawn after Moliere's manner, and that an eafy and natural vein of humour ran through the whole.

I do not queftion but the reader will difcover this, and fee many beauties that efcaped the audience; the touches being too delicate for every tafte in a popular affembly. My bro-ther-fharers were of opinion, at the firft rea-ding of it, that it was like a picture in which, the ftrokes were not ftrong enough to appear at a diftance. As it is not in the common way of writing, the approbation was at firft doubtful, but has rifen every time it has been acted, and has given an opportunity in feveral of its parts for as juft and good action as ever I faw on the ftage.

The reader will confider that I fpeak here, not as the author, but as the patentee. Which is, perhaps, the reafon why I am not diffufe in the praifes of the play, left I fhould feem like a man who cries up his own wares only to draw in cuftomers.

RICHARD STEELE.

P R O-

IN this grave age, when comedies are few,
We crave your patronage for one that's new;
Though 'twere poor stuff, yet bid the author fair,
And let the scarceness recommend the ware.
Long have your ears been fill'd with tragic parts,
Blood and blank verse have harden'd all your hearts;
If e'er you smile 'tis at some party strokes,
Round heads and wooden shoes are standing jokes;
The same conceit gives claps and hisses birth,
You're grown such politicians in your mirth!
For once we try (though 'tis I own unsafe,)
To please you all, and make both parties laugh.

Our author, anxious for his fame to night,
And bashful in his first attempt to write,
Lies cautiously obscure and unreveal'd,
Like antient actors in a mask conceal'd,
Censure, when no man knows who writes the play,
Were much good malice merely thrown away.
The mighty critics, will not blast, for shame,
A raw young thing, who dares not tell his name:
Good-natur'd judges will th' unknown defend,
And fear to blame, lest they should hurt a friend:
Each wit may praise it, for his own dear sake,
And hint he writ it, if the thing should take.
But if you're rough, and use him like a dog,
Depend upon it——he'll remain incog.
If you should hiss, he swears he'll hiss as high,
And, like a culprit, join the hue-and-cry.

If cruel men are still averse to spare
These scenes, they fly for refuge to the fair.
Though with a ghost our comedy be heighten'd,
Ladies, upon my word, you shan't be frighten'd;
O, 'tis a ghost that scorns to be uncivil;
A well-spread, lusty, jointure-hunting devil;
An am'rous ghost, that's faithful, fond and true,
Made of flesh and blood——as much as you.
Then every evening come in flocks, undaunted,
We never think this house is too much haunted.

Dramatis

Dramatis Personæ.

Sir George Trueman,	Mr Wilks.
Tinsel,	Mr Cibber.
Fantome, the Drummer,	Mr Mills.
Vellum, Sir George's steward,	Mr Johnson.
Butler,	Mr Penkethman.
Coachman,	Mr Miller.
Gardiner,	Mr Norris.
Lady Trueman,	Mrs Oldfield.
Abigal,	Mrs Saunders.

THE

THE

DRUMMER;

OR THE

HAUNTED·HOUSE.

ACT I. SCENE I.

A Great Hall.

Enter the Butler, Coachman, and Gardiner.

Butl. THERE came another coach to town laſt night, that brought a gentleman to enquire about this ſtrange noiſe, we hear in the houſe. This ſpirit will bring a power of cuſtom to the George——If ſo be he continues his pranks, I deſign to ſell a pot of ale, and ſet up the ſign of the drum.

Coachm. I'll give Madam warning that's flat—I've always liv'd in ſober families. I'll not diſparage myſelf to be a ſervant in a houſe that is haunted.

Gard. I'll e'en marry Nell, and rent a bit of ground of my own, if both of you leave Madam ; not but that Madam's a very good woman—If Mrs Abigal did not ſpoil her——come, here's her health.

Butl. It's a very hard thing to be a butler in a houſe that is diſturb'd. He made ſuch a racket in the cellar laſt night, that I'm afraid he'll ſour all the beer in my barrels.

Coachm. Why then, John, we ought to take it off as faſt as we can, here's to you—he rattled ſo loud under the tiles laſt night, that I verily thought the houſe wou'd have fallen over our heads. I durſt not go up into the cock loft this morning, if I had not got one of the maids to go along with me.

Gard. I thought I heard him in one of my bed·poſts —I marvel, John, how he gets into the houſe when all the gates are ſhut.

Butl. Why look ye, Peter, your ſpirit will creep you

into

into an augre-hole : he'll whisk you through a key-hole, without so much as jussling against one of the wards.

Coachm. Poor Madam is mainly frighted, that's certain, and verily believes 'tis my master that was kill'd in the last campaign.

Butl. Out of all manner of question, Robin, 'tis Sir George. Mrs Abigal is of opinion it can be none but his Honour; he always lov'd the wars, and you know was mightily pleas'd from a child with the music of a drum.

Gard. I wonder his body was never found after the battle.

Butl. Found ! Why, you fool, is not his body here about the house ? Dost thou think he can beat his drum without hands and arms ?

Coachm. 'Tis master as sure as I stand here alive, and I verily believe I saw him last night in the town-close.

Gard. Ay ! how did he appear ?

Coachm. Like a white horse.

Butl. Pho, Robin, I tell ye he has never appear'd yet but in the shape of the sound of a drum.

Coachm. This makes one almost afraid of one's own shadow. As I was walking from the stable t'other night without my lanthorn, I fell a cross a beam, that lay in my way, and faith my heart was in my mouth——I thought I had stumbled over a spirit.

Butl. Thou might'st as well have stumbled over a straw ; why, a spirit is such a little little thing, that I have heard a man, who was a great scholar, say, that he'll dance a Lancashire horn pipe upon the point of a needle —As I sat in the pantry last night counting my spoons, the candle methought burnt blue, and the spay'd bitch look'd as if she saw something.

Coachm. Ay, poor cur, she's almost frighten'd out of her wits.

Gard. Ay, I warrant ye, she hears him many a time and often when we don't.

Butl. My Lady must have him laid, that's certain, whatever it cost her.

Gard I fancy when one goes to market, one might hear of some body that can make a spell.

Coachm. Why may not the parson of our parish lay him ?

Butl.

Butl. No, no, no, our parson cannot lay him.

Coachm. Why not he as well as another man?

Butl. Why, ye fool, he is not qualified—he has not taken the oaths.

Gard. Why d'ye think John, that the spirit wou'd take the law of him—faith, I could tell you one way to drive him off.

Coachm. How's that?

Gard. I'll tell you immediately [*drinks*]—I fancy Mrs Abigal might scold him out of the house.

Coachm. Ay, she has a tongue that would drown his drum if any thing cou'd.

Butl. Pugh, this is all froth! you understand nothing of the matter—the next time it makes a noise, I'll tell you what ought to be done—I wou'd have the steward speak Latin to it.

Coachm. Ay, that wou'd do, if the steward had but courage.

Gard. There you have it—He's a fearful man. If I had as much learning as he, and I met the ghost, I'd tell him his own! but alack what can one of us poor men do with a spirit, that can neither write nor read?

Butl. Thou art always cracking and boasting, Peter; thou dost not know what mischief it might do thee, if such a silly dog as thee should offer to speak to it. For ought I know, he might flea thee alive, and make parchment of thy skin to cover his drum with.

Gard. A fiddle stick! tell not me—I fear nothing; not I! I never did harm in my life, I never committed murder.

Butl. I verily believe thee, keep thy temper, Peter; after supper we'll drink each of us a double mug, and then let come what will.

Gard. Why that's well said, John, an honest man that is not quite sober, has nothing to fear——Here's to ye—why how if he shou'd come this minute, here wou'd I stand. Ha! what noise is that?

Butl. and *Coachm.* Ha! where!

Gard. The devil! the devil! Oh no, 'tis Mrs Abigal.

Butl. Ay, faith! 'tis she; 'tis Mrs Abigal! a good mistake! 'tis Mrs Abigal.

Enter.

Enter Abigal.

Abig. Here are your drunken fots for you! Is this a time to be a guzzling, when gentry are come to the house! why don't you lay your cloth? How come you out of the stables? Why are not you at work in your garden?

Gard. Why, yonder's the fine Londoner and Madam fetching a walk together, and methought they look'd as if they should fay they had rather have my room than my company.

Butl. And fo forfooth being all three met together, we are doing our endeavours to drink this fame drummer out of our heads.

Gard. For you muft know, Mrs Abigal, we are all of opinion that one can't be a match for him, unlefs one be as drunk as a drum.

Coachm. I am refolved to give Madam warning to hire herfelf another coachman; for I came to ferve my mafter, d'ye fee, while he was alive, but do fuppofe that he has no farther occafion for a coach, now he walks.

Butl. Truly, Mrs Abigal, I muft needs fay, that this fame fpirit is a very odd fort of a body, after all, to fright Madam and his old fervants at this rate.

Gard. And truly, Mrs Abigal, I muft needs fay, I ferv'd my mafter contentedly, while he was living; but I will ferve no man living, (that is, no man that is not living) without double wages.

Abig. Ay, 'tis fuch cowards as you that go about with idle ftories to difgrace the houfe. and bring fo many ftrangers about it; you firft frighten yourfelves, and then your neighbours.

Gard. Frightned? I fcorn your words. Frighten'd quoth·a!

Abig. What you fot! are you grown pot·valiant?

Gard. Frighten'd with a drum! that's a good one! 'twill do us no harm, I'll anfwer for it. It will bring no bloodfhed along with it, take my word. It founds as like a train band drum as ever I heard in my life.

Butl. Pr'ytheee, Peter, don't be fo prefumptuous.

Abig. Well, thefe drunken rogues take it as I could wifh.   [*Afide.*
Gard.

Gard. I scorn to be frightned, now I'm in for't! if old dub-a-bub should come into the room, I wou'd take him——

Butl. Pr'ythee hold thy tongue.

Gard. I wou'd take him.——

[*The drum beats, the gardiner endeavours to get off, and falls.*

Butl. and *Coachm.* Speak to it, Mrs Abigal.

Gard. Spare my life, and take all I have.

Coachm. Make off, make off, good butler, and let us go hide ourselves in the cellar. [*They all run off.*

Abigal *sola.*

Abig. So, now the coast is clear, I may venture to call out my drummer—But first let me shut the door, left we be surprized. Mr Fantome! Mr Fantome! [*He beats.*] Nay, nay, pray come out, the enemy's fled—I must speak with you immediately —don't stay to beat a parley.

[*The back scene opens and discovers Fantome with a drum.*

Fant. Dear Mrs Nabby, I have overheard all that has been said, and find thou hast managed this thing so well, that I cou'd take thee in my arms, and kiss thee—if my drum did not stand in my way.

Abig. Well, O' my conscience, you are the merriest ghost! and the very picture of Sir George Trueman.

Fant. There you flatter me, Mrs Abigal: Sir George had that freshness in his looks, that we men of the town cannot come up to.

Abig. Oh! death may have alter'd you, you know—besides, you must consider, you lost a great deal of blood in the battle.

Fant. Ay, that's right; let me look never so pale, this cut cross my forehead will keep me in countenance.

Abig. 'Tis just such a one as my master receiv'd from a cursed French trooper, as my Lady's letter inform'd her.

Fant. It happens luckily that this suit of cloaths of Sir George's fits me so well: I think— I can't fail hiting the air of a man with whom I was so long acquainted.

Abig.

Abig. You are the very man--I vow I almost ftart when I look upon you.

Fant But what good will this do me, if I muft remain invifible ?

Abig. Pray what good did your being vifible do you ? The fair Mr Fantome thought no woman cou'd with-ftand hir.—but when you were feen by my lady in your proper perfon, after fhe had taken a full furvey of you, and heard al' the pretty things you cou'd fay, fhe very civilly difmifs'd you for the fake of this empty, noify creature Tinfel. She fancies you have been gone from hence this fortnight.

Fant. Why really I love thy Lady fo well, that tho' I had no hopes of gaining her for myfelf, I cou'd not bear to fee her given to another, efpecially fuch a wretch as Tinfel.

Abig. Well, tell me truly, Mr Fantome, have you not a great opinion of my fidelity to my dear Lady, that I would not fuffer her to be deluded in this manner, for lefs than a thoufand pound ?

Fant. Thou art always remembring me of my pro-mife—thou fhalt have it, if thou canft bring our project to bear; doft not know that ftories of ghofts and appa-ritions generally end in a pot of money.

Abig. Why, truly now Mr Fantome, I fhould think myfelf a very bad woman, if I had done what I do, for a farthing lefs.

Fant. Dear Abigal, how I admire thy virtue !

Abig. No, no, Mr Fantome, I defy the worft of my enemies to fay I love mifchief for mifchief's fake.

Fant. But is thy Lady perfuaded that I am the ghoft of her deceafed husband ?

Abig. I endeavour to make her believe fo, and tell her every time your drum rattles, that her husband is chiding her for entertaining this new love.

Fant. Pry'thee make ufe of all thy art, for I am tir'd to death with ftrowling round this wide old houfe, like a rat behind a wainfcot.

Abig. Did not I tell you, 'twas the pureft place in the world for you to play your tricks in ? there's none of the family that knows every hole and corner in it, befides myfelf.

Fant.

Fant. Ah Mrs Abigal! you have had your intrigues.

Abig. For you muſt know, when I was a romping young girl, I was a mighty lover of *hide and ſeek.*

Fant. I believe, by this time, I am as well acquainted with the houſe as yourſelf.

Abig. You are very much miſtaken, Mr Fantome; but no matter for that; here is to be your ſtation to night. This is a place unknown to any one living beſides myſelf, ſince the death of the joiner; who, you muſt underſtand, being a lover of mine, contrived the wainſcot to move to and fro, in the manner that you find it. I deſign'd it for a wardrobe for my Lady's caſt cloaths. Oh! the ſtomachers, ſtays, petticoats, commodes, laced ſhoes, and good things that I have had in it—pray take care you don't break the cherry-brandy bottle that ſtands up in the carner.

Fant. Well, Mrs Abigal, I hire your cloſet of you but for this one night——a thouſand pound you know is a very good rent.

Abig. Well, get you gone; you have ſuch a way with you, there's no denying you any thing!

Fant. I'm a thinking how Tinſel will ſtare when he ſees me come out of the wall; for I'm reſolv'd to make my appearance to night.

Abig. Get you in, get you in, my Lady's at the door.

Fant. Pray take care ſhe does not keep me up ſo late as ſhe did laſt night, or depend upon it I'll beat the Tatoo.

Abig. I'm undone! I'm undone—[*As he is going in.*] Mr Fantome, Mr Fantome, you have put the thouſand pound bond into my brother's hands.

Fant. Thou ſhalt have it, I tell thee, thou ſhalt have it. [*Fantome goes in.*

Abig. No more words—vaniſh, vaniſh.

Enter Lady.

Abig. [*opening the door.*] Oh, dear Madam, was it you that made ſuch a knocking? my heart does ſo beat—I vow you have frighted me to death—I thought verily it had been the drummer.

Lady. I have been ſhowing the garden to Mr Tinſel; he's

he's moſt inſufferably witty upon us about the ſtory of the drum.

Abig. Indeed, Madam, he's a very looſe man ! I'm afraid 'tis he that hinders my poor maſter from reſting in his grave.

Lady. Well ! an infidel is ſuch a novelty in the country, that I am reſolv'd to divert myſelf a day or two at leaſt with the oddneſs of his converſation.

Abig. Ah, Madam ! the drum began to beat in the houſe as ſoon as ever this creature was admitted to viſit you. All the while Mr Fantome made his addreſſes to you, there was not a mouſe ſtirring in the family more than uſed to be.

Lady. This baggage has ſome deſign upon me, more than I can yet diſcover. [*aſide.*]—Mr Fantome was always thy favourite.

Abig. Ay, and ſhould have been yours too, by my conſent ! Mr Fantome was not ſuch a ſlight fantaſtic thing as this is.—Mr Fantome was the beſt built man one ſhou'd ſee in a ſummer's day ! Mr Fantome was a man of honour, and lov'd you ! poor ſoul ! how he ſigh'd when he has talked to me of my hard-hearted lady— —Well ! I had as lief as a thouſand pounds you would marry Mr Fantome !

Lady. To tell thee truly, I lov'd him well enough till I found he lov'd me ſo much. But Mr Tinſel makes his court to me with ſo much neglect and indifference, and with ſuch an agreeable ſaucineſs—not that I ſay I'll marry him.

Abig. Marry him, queth a ! no, if you ſhould, you'll be awaken'd ſooner than married couples generally are —— you'll quickly have a drum at your window.

Lady. I'll hide my contempt of Tinſel, for once, if it be but to ſee what this wench drives at. [*aſide.*

Abig. Why, ſuppoſe your buſband, after this fair warning he has given you, ſhou'd ſound you an alarm at midnight ; then open your curtains with a face as pale as my apron, and cry out with a hollow voice, what doſt thou do in bed with this ſpindle ſhanked fellow ?

Lady. Why wilt thou needs have it to be my husband? he never had any reaſon to be offended at me. I always

ways lov'd him while he was living, and should prefer
him to any man, were he so still. Mr Tinsel is inded very
idle in his talk, but I fancy, Abigal, a discreet woman
might reform him.

Abig. That's a likely matter indeed ? did you ever
hear of a woman who had power over a man when she
was his wife, that had none while she was his mistress !
oh ! there's nothing in the world improves a man in his
complaisance like marriage !

Lady. He is indeed, at present, too familiar in his conversation.

Abig. Familiar ! Madam, in troth, he's downright
rude.

Lady. But that you know, Abigal, shows he has no
dissimulation in him——then he is apt to jest a little too
much upon grave subjects.

Abig. Grave subjects ! he jests upon the church.

Lady But that you know, Abigal, may be only to
shew his wit——then it must be own'd he's extremely
talkative.

Abig. Talkative d'ye call it ! he's downright impertinent.

Lady. But that you know, Abigal, is a sign he has
been us'd to good company——then indeed he is very
positive.

Abig. Positive ! why he contradicts you in every thing
you say.

Lady. But then you know, Abigal, he has been educated at the Inns of Court.

Abig. A blessed education indeed ! it has made him
forget his catechism !

Lady. You talk as if you hated him.

Abig. You talk as if you lov'd him.

Lady. Hold your tongue ! here he comes.

Enter Tinsel.

Tins. My dear widow !

Abig. My dear widow ! marry come up !   [*aside.*

Lady. Let him alone, Abigal, so long as he does not
call me my dear wife, there's no harm done.

Tins. I have been most ridiculously diverted since I
left you—your servants have made a convert of my boo-
by.

by. His head is so filled with this foolish story of a drummer, that I expect the rogue will be afraid, hereafter
to go upon a message by moon light.

Lady. Ah, Mr Tinsel. what a loss of billet-doux would
that be to many a fine Lady!

Abig. Then you still believe this to be a foolish story?
I thought my Lady had told you, that she had heard it
herself.

Tins. Ha, ha, ha!

Abig. Why, you would not persuade us out of our
senses.

Tins. Ha ha, ha!

Abig. There's manners for you, Madam.   [*aside.*

Lady. Admirably rally'd! that laugh is unanswera-
ble! now I'll be hang'd if you could forbear being witty upon me, if I should tell you I heard it no longer a-
go than last night.

Tins. Fancy!

Lady. But what if I should tell you my maid was with
me!

Tins. Vapours! vapours! pray. my dear widow, will
you answer me one question?—had you ever this noise
of a drum in your head, all the while your husband was
living?

Lady. And pray, Mr Tinsel, will you let me ask you
another question? do you think we can hear in the country, as well as you do in town?

Tins. Believe me, Madam, I could prescribe you a
cure for these imaginations.

Abig. Don't tell my lady of imaginations, Sir, I have
heard it myself.

Tins. Hark thee, child—art thou not an old-maid?

Abig. Sir, if I am, it is mine own fault.

Tins. Whims! freaks! megrims! indeed Mrs Abigal.

Abig. Marry, Sir, by your talk one would believe you
thought every thing that was good is a megrim.

Lady. Why truly I don't very well understand what
you mean by your doctrine to me in the garden just now,
that every thing we saw was made by chance.

Abig. A very pretty subject indeed for a lover to divert
his mistress with.

Abig.

Lady. But I suppose that was only a taste of the conversation you would entertain me with after marriage.

Tinf. Oh I shall then have time to read you such lectures of motions, atoms, and nature—that you shall learn to think as freely as the best of us, and be convinced in less than a month, that all about us is chance work.

Lady. You are a very complaisant person indeed; and so you would make your court to me, by persuading me that I was made by chance!

Tinf. Ha, ha, ha! well said my dear! Why faith, thou wert a very lucky hit, that's certain.

Lady. Pray, Mr Tinfel, where did you learn this odd way of talking?

Tinf. Ah, widow, 'tis your country innocence makes you think it an odd way of talking.

Lady. Tho' you give no credit to stories of apparitions, I hope you believe there are such things as spirits!

Tinf. Simplicity!

Abig. I fancy you don't believe women have souls, d'ye Sir!

Tinf. Foolish enough!

Lady. I vow, Mr Tinfel, I'm afraid malicious people will say I'm in love with an atheist.

Tinf. Oh, my dear, that's an old fashion'd word—I'm a free-thinker, child.

Abig. I am sure you are a free speaker.

Lady. Really, Mr Tinfel, considering that you are so fine a Gentleman, I'm amaz'd where you got all this learning! I wonder it has not spoil'd your breeding.

Tinf. To tell you the truth, I have not time to look into these dry matters myself, but I'm convinced by four or five learned men, whom I sometimes over hear at a coffeehouse I frequent, that our forefathers were a pack of asses, that the world has been in an error for some thousands of years and that all the people upon earth, excepting those two or three worthy Gentlemen, are impos'd upon, cheated, bubbled, abus'd bamboozled—

Abig. Madam, how can you hear such a profligate? he talks like the London prodigal.

Lady. Why really I'm a thinking, if there be no such
things

' ings as spirits, a woman has no occasion, for marrying
——she need not be afraid to lie by herself.

Tinf. Ah! my dear! are husbands good for nothing
but to frighten away spirits? didst thou think I could not
instruct thee in several other comforts of matrimony?

Lady. Ah! but you are a man of so much knowledge
that you would always be laughing at my ignorance—you
learned men are so apt to despise one!

Tinf. No, child! I'd teach thee my principles, thou
should'st be as wise as I am—in a week's time.

Lady. Do you think your principles would make a woman the better wife?

Tinf. Pr'ythee, widow don't be queer.

Lady. I love a gay temper, but I would not have you
rally things that are serious.

Tinf. Well enough, faith! where's the jest of rallying
any thing else!

Abig. Ah, Madam, did you ever hear Mr Fantome
talk at this rate?   [*aside.*

Tinf. But where's this ghost! the son of a whore of a
drummer? I'd fain hear him, methinks.

Abig. Pray, Madam, don't suffer him to give the ghost
such ill language, especially when you have reason to believe it is my master.

Tinf. That's well enough faith, Nab; dost thou
think thy master is so unreasonable, as to continue his
claim to his relict after his bones are laid? pray, widow,
remember the words of your contract, you have fulfill'd
them to a tittle———did not you marry Sir George to
the tune of, '*till death us do part?*

Lady. I must not hear Sir George's memory treated in
so slight a manner—this fellow must have been at some
pains to make himself such a finish'd coxcomb. [*aside.*

Tinf. Give me but possession of your person, and I'll whirl
you up to town for a winter, and cure you at once. Oh!
I have known many a country Lady come to London
with frightful stories of the hall house being haunted, of
fairies, spirits, and witches; that by the time she had
seen a comedy, play'd at an assembly, and ambled in a
ball or two, has been so little afraid of bugbears, that she
has ventur'd home in a chair at all hours of the night.

Abig.

Abig. Hum—ſauce box ⸢*aſide.*

Tinſ. 'Tis the ſolitude of the country that creates theſe whimſies ; there was never ſuch a thing as a ghoſt heard of at London, except in the play-houſe—Oh we'd paſs all our time in London. 'Tis the ſcene of pleaſure and diverſions, where there's ſomething to amuſe you every hour of the day. Life's not life in the country.

Lady. Well then, you have an opportunity of ſhowing the ſincerity of that love to me which you profeſs. You may give a proof that you have an affection to my perſon, not my jointure.

Tinſ. Your jointure ! how can you think me ſuch a dog ! but child, won't your jointure be the ſame thing in London as in the country ?

Lady. No, you're deceiv'd ! you muſt know it is ſettled on me by marriage articles, on conditions that I live in this old manſion-houſe, and keep it up in repair.

Tinſ. How !

Abig That's well put, Madam.

Tinſ. Why faith I have been looking upon this houſe, and think it is the prettieſt habitation I ever ſaw in my life.

Lady. Ay, but then this cruel drum !

Tinſ. Something ſo venerable in it !

Lady. Ay, but the drum !

Tinſ. For my part, I like this Gothic way of building better than any of your new orders—it would be a thouſand pities it ſhould fall to ruin.

Lady. Ay, but the drum !

Tinſ. How pleaſantly we two could paſs our time in this delicious ſituation. Our lives would be a continu'd dream of happineſs. Come, faith, widow, let's go upon the leads and take a view of the country.

Lady. Ay, but the drum ! the drum !

Tinſ. My dear, take my word for't 'tis all fancy, beſides, ſhou'd he drum in thy very bed-chamber, I ſhould only hug thee the cloſer.

Claſp'd in the folds of love, I'd meet my doom,
And act my joys, tho' thunder ſhock the room.

A C T

ACT II.   SCENE I.

SCENE *opens, and discovers* Vellum *in this office, and a letter in his hand.*

VELLUM.

THIS letter astonisheth ; may I believe may own eyes—or rather my spectacles—*To* Humphrey Vellum, Esq; Steward to the Lady Trueman.

Vellum,

'I Doubt not but you will be glad to hear your master
' is alive, and designs to be with you in half an hour.
' The report of my being slain in the Netherlands, has, I
' find, produced some disorders in my family. I am now
' at the George-Inn ; if an old man with a grey beard,
' in a black cloke, enquires after you, give him admit-
' tance.   He passes for a conjurer, but is really

Your faithful friend,

G. Trueman.

P. S. Let this be a secret, and you shall find your ac-
' count in it.'

This amazeth me ! and yet the reasons why I should believe he is still living are manifold—First, because this has
often been the case of other military adventurers.

Secondly, because the news of his death was first pub-
lish'd in Dyer's Letter.

Thirdly, Because this letter can be written by none but
himself——I know his hand, and manner of spelling,

Fourthly,——

Enter Butler.

Butl. Sir, here's a strange old Gentleman that asks for
you ; he says he's a conjurer, but he looks very suspici-
ous ; I wish he ben't a Jesuit.

Vel. Admit him immediately.

Butl. I wish he ben't a Jesuit ; but he says he's nothing but a conjurer.

Bring

Vel. He fays right——he is no more than a conjurer. Bring him in, and withdraw.   [*Exit Butler.*

And fourthly, as I was faying, becaufe——

Enter Butler *with* Sir George.

Butl. Sir, here in the conjurer——what a devilifh long beard he has ! I warrant it has been growing thefe hundred years.   [*afide. Exit.*

Sir Geo. Dear Vellum, you have received my letter ; but before we proceed lock the door.

Vel. It is his voice.   [*fhuts the door.*

Sir Geo. In the next place help me off with this cumberfome cloke.

Vel. It is his fhape.

Sir Geo. So, now lay my beard upon the table.

Vel. [*After having look'd on Sir George thro' bis fpectacles*] It is his face, every lineament !

Sir Geo. Well, now I have put off the conjurer and the old man, I can talk to thee more at my eafe.

Vel. Believe me, my good mafter, I am as much rejoiced to fee you alive, as I was upon the day you were born. Your name was in all the news-papers, in the lift of thefe that were flain.

Sir Geo. We have not time to be particular. I fhall only tell thee in general, that I was taken prifoner in the battle, and was under clofe confinement for feveral months. Upon my releafe, I was refolved to furprize my wife with the news of my being alive. I know, Vellum, you are a perfon of fo much penetration, that I need not ufe any further arguments to convince you that I am fo.

Vel. I am—and moreover, I queftion not but your good Lady will likewife be convinc'd of it. Her honour is a difcerning Lady.

Sir Geo. I'm only afraid fhe fhou'd be convinc'd of it to her forrow. Is not fhe pleafed with her imaginary widow-hood ? tell me truly, was fhe afflicted at the report of my death ?

Vel. Sorely.

Sir Geo. How long did her grief laft ?

Vel. Longer than I have known any widow's—at leaft three days.

Sir

Sir Geo. Three days, fay'ft thou ? three whole days ? I'm afraid thou flattereft me !——O woman ! woman !

Vel. Grief is twofold.

Sir Geo. This blockhead is as methodical as ever—but I know he's honeft.   [*afide.*

Vel. There is a real grief, and there is a methodical grief ; fhe was drown'd in tears till fuch time as the Taylor had made her widow's weeds—indeed they became her.

Sir Geo. Became her !' and was that her comfort ? truly a moft feafonable confolation !

Vel. But I muft needs fay fhe paid a due regard to your memory, and could not forbear weeping when fhe faw company.

Sir Geo. That was kind indeed ! I find fhe griev'd with a deal of good breeding. But how comes this gang of lovers about her ?

Vel. Her jointure is confiderable.

Sir Geo. How this fool torments me !   [*afide.*

Vel. Her perfon is amiable——

Sir Geo. Death !   [*afide.*

Vel. But her character is unblemifh'd. She has been as virtuous in your abfence as a Penelope——

Sir Geo. And has had as many fuitors ?

Vel. Several have made their overtures.

Sir Geo. Several !

Vel. But fhe has rejected all.

Sir Geo. There thou reviv'ft me—but what means this Tinfel ? are his vifits acceptable ?

Vel. He is young.

Sir Geo. Does fhe liften to him ?

Vel. He is gay.

Sir Geo. Sure fhe could never entertain a thought of marrying fuch a coxcomb !

Vel He is not ill made

Sir Geo. Are the vows and proteftations that paft between us come to this ! I can't bear the thought of it ! is Tinfel the man defign'd for my worthy fucceffor ?

Vel You do not confider that you have been dead thefe fourteen months——

Sir Geo. Was there ever fuch a dog ?   [*afide.*
                                                  Vel.

Vel. And I have often heard her say, that she must never expect to find a second Sir George Trueman—— meaning your honour.

Sir Geo. I think she lov'd me ; but I must search into this story of the drummer before I discover myself to her. I have put on this habit of a conjurer, in order to introduce myself. It must be your business to recommend me as a most profound person, that by my great knowledge in the curious arts can silence the drummer, and dispossess the house.

Vel. I am going to lay my accounts before my Lady, and I will endeavour to prevail upon her honour to admit the trial of your art.

Sir Geo. I have scarce heard of any of these stories that did not arise from a love intrigue——Amours raise as many ghosts as murders.

Vel Mrs Abigal endeavours to persuade us, that 'tis your honour who troubles the house.

Sir Geo. That convinces me 'tis a cheat, for I think, Vellum, I may be pretty well assur'd it is not me.

Vel. I am apt to think so truly. Ha——ha——ha ?

Sir Geo. Abigal had always an ascendant over her Lady, and if there is any trick in this matter, depend upon it she is at the bottom of it. I'll be hang'd if this ghost be not one of Abigal's familiars.

Vel. Mrs Abigal has of late been very mysterious.

Ser Geo. I fancy, Vellum, thou could'st worm it out of her. I know formerly there was an amour between you.

Vel. Mrs Abigal hath her allurements, and she knows I have pick'd up a competency in you honour's service.

Sir Geo. If thou hast, all I ask of thee in return is, that thou would'st immediately renew thy addresses to her. Cox her up. Thou hast such a silver tongue, Vellum, as 'twill be impossible for her to withstand. Besides, she is so very a woman, that she'll like thee the better for giving her the pleasure of telling a secret. In short, wheedle her out of it, and I shall act by the advice which thou givest me.

Vel. Mrs Abigal was never deaf to me, when I talked upon that subject. I will take an opportunity of addresfing myfelf to her in the moft pathetic manner.

Sir Geo. In the mean time lock me up in your office, and bring me word what fuccefs you have ——well, fure I am the firft that ever was employ'd to lay himfelf.

Vel. You act indeed a threefold part in this houfe ; you are a ghoft, a conjurer, and my ho noured mafter Sir George Trueman ; he, he, he ! you will pardon me for being jocular.

Sir Geo. O, Mr Vellum, with all my heart. You know I love you men of wit and humour. Be as merry as thou pleafeft, fo thou doft thy bufinefs. [*Mimicking him*] You will remember, Vellum, your commiffion is two-fold, firft to gain admiffion for me to your Lady, and fecondly to get the fecret out of Abigal.

Vel. It fufficeth.   [*The fcene fhuts.*

Enter Lady *fola.*

Lady. Women who have been happy in a firft marriage, are the moft apt to venture upon a fecond. But for my part I had a husband fo every way fuited to my inclinations, that I muft entirely forget him, before I can like another man. I have now been a widow but fourteen months, and have had twice as many lovers, all of 'em perfect admirers of my perfon, but paffionately in love with my jointure. I think it is a revenge I owe my fex to make an example of this worthlefs tribe of fellows, who grow impudent, drefs themfelves fine, and fancy we are obliged to provide for 'em. But of all my captives, Mr Tinfel is the moft extraordinary in his kind. I hope the diverfion I give myfelf with him is unblameable. I'm fure 'tis neceffary to turn my thoughts off from the memory of that dear man, who has been the greateft happinefs and affliction of my life. My heart would be a prey to melancholy, if I did not find thefe innocent methods of relieving it. But here comes Abigal, I muft teaze the baggage, for I find fhe has taken it into her head that I am intirely at her difpofal.

Enter Abigal.

Abig. Madam ! Madam ! yonder's Mr Tinfel has as good as taken poffeffion of your houfe. Marry, he fays, he muft have Sir George's apartment enlarg'd : for truly fays he, I hate to be ftraitned. Nay, he was fo impudent

dent as to ꜠hew me the chamber where he intends to con-
꜠ummate, as he calls it.

Lady. Well ! he's a wild fellow.

Abig. Indeed he's a very ꜠ad man, Madam.

Lady. He's young, Abigal ; 'tis a thou꜠and pities he
꜠hould be lo꜠t ; I ꜠hould be mighty glad to reform him.

Abig. Reform him ! marry hang him !

Lady. Has not he a great deal of life !

Abig. Ay, enough to make your heart ake.

Lady. I dare ꜠ay thou think'꜠t him a very agreeable
fellow.

Abig. He thinks him꜠elf ꜠o, I'll an꜠wer for him.

Lady. He's very good natur'd.

Abig. He ought to be ꜠o, for he's very ꜠illy.

Lady. Do꜠t thou think he loves me ?

Abig. Mr Fantome did, I am ꜠ure.

Lady. With what raptures he talk'd !

Abig. Yes, 'twas in prai꜠e of your jointure-hou꜠e.

Lady. He has kept bad company.

Abig. They mu꜠t be very bad indeed, if they were
wor꜠e than him꜠elf.

Lady. I have a ꜠trong fancy a good woman might reform him.

Abig. It would be a fine experiment, if it ꜠hould not
꜠ucceed.

Lady. Well Abigal, we'll talk of that another time ;
here comes the Steward, I have no further occa꜠ion for
you at pre꜠ent.   [*Exit Abigal.*

Enter Vellum.

Vel. Madam, is your ho-nour at lei꜠ure to look into
the accounts of the la꜠t week ? they ri꜠e very high—hou꜠e-
keeping is chargeable in a hou꜠e that is haunted.

Lady. How comes that to pa꜠s ? I hope the drum neither eats nor drinks ? but read your account, Vellum.

Vel. [*Putting on and off his ꜠pectacles in this ꜠cene*] A
hog꜠head and a half of ale—it is not for the gho꜠t's drinking——but your ho-nour's ꜠ervants ꜠ay they mu꜠t have
꜠omething to keep up their courage again꜠t this ꜠trange
noi꜠e. They tell me they expect a double quantity of
                                              malt

C

malt in their small beer, so long as the house continues in this condition.

Lady. At this rate they'll take care to be frighten'd all the year round, I'll answer for 'em. But go on.

Vel. Item. Two sheep, and a—where is the ox?—Oh, here I have him—and an ox—your ho-nour must always have a piece of cold beef in the house for the entertainment of so many strangers, who come from all parts to hear this drum. *Item,* Bread, ten peck loaves—they cannot eat beef without bread—*Item,* three barrels of table-beer—they must drink with their meat.

Lady. Sure no woman in England has a Steward that makes such ingenious comments on his works.   [*aside.*

Vel. Item, To Mr Tinsel's servants five bottles of port wine—it was by your ho-nour's order—*Item,* three bottles of sack for the use of Mrs Abigal.

Lady. I suppose that was by your own order.

Vel. We have been long friends, we are your honour's ancient servants; sack is an innocent cordial, and gives her spirit to chide the servants, when they are tardy in their business; he, he, he! pardon me for being jocular.

Lady. Well I see you'll come together at last.

Vel. Item, A dozen pound of watch-lights for the use of the servants.

Lady. For the use of the servants! What, are the rogues afraid of sleeping in the dark! what an unfortunate woman am I! this is such a particular distress, it puts me to my wits end. Vellum, what would you advise me to do?

Vel. Madam your ho-nour has two points to consider. *Imprimis,* To retrench these extravagant expences, which so many strangers bring upon you—*Secondly,* To clear the house of this invisible drummer.

Lady. This learned division leaves me just as wise as I was. But how must we bring these two points to bear?

Vel. I beseech your ho nour to give me the hearing.

Lady. I do. But pr'ythee take pity on me, and be not tedious·

Vel. I will be concise. There is a certain person arriv'd this morning, an aged man of a venerable aspect, and of a long hoary beard, that reaches down to his girdle.

The

The common people call him a wizard, a white witch, conjurer, a cunning man, a necromancer, a ———

Lady. No matter for his titles. But what of all this?

Vel. Give me the hearing, good my lady. He pretends to great skill in the occult sciences, and is come hither upon the rumour of this drum. If one may believe him he knows the secret of laying ghosts, or of quieting houses that are haunted.

Lady. Pho, these are idle stories to amuse the country people, this can do us no good.

Vel. It can do us no harm, my Lady.

Lady. I dare say thou dost not believe there is any thing in it thyself.

Vel. I cannot say, I do; there is no danger however in the experiment. Let him try his skill; if it should succeed, we are rid of the drum; if it should not, we may tell the world that it has, and by that means at least get out of this expensive way of living: so that it must turn to your advantage one way or another.

Lady. I think you argue very rightly. But where is the man? I would fain see him. He must be a curiosity.

Vel. I have already discoursed him, and he is to be with me in my office, half an hour hence. He asks nothing for his pains, till he has done his work—no cure, no money.

Lady. That circumstance, I must confess, would make one believe there is more in his art than one would imagine. Pray Vellum, go and fetch him hither immediately.

Vel. I am gone. He shall be forth coming forthwith.
[*Exeunt.*

Enter Butler, Coachman, *and* Gardiner.

Butl. Rare news, my lads, rare news!

Gard. What's the matter! hast thou got any more tales for us?

Butl. No, 'tis better than that.

Coach. Is there another stranger come to the house?

Butl. Ay, such a stranger as will make all our lives easy.

Gard. What! is he a Lord?

Butl. A Lord! nothing like it.——He's a conjurer.

Coach. A conjurer! what, is he come a wooing to my Lady?

Butl

Butl. No, no, you fool, he's come on purpose to lay the spirit.

Coach. Ay marry, that's good news indeed; but where is he?

Butl. He's lock'd up with the steward in his office, they are laying their heads together very close. I fancy they are casting a figure.

Gard. Pr'ythee John, what sort of a creature is a conjurer?

Butl. Why he's made much as other men are, if it was not for his long grey beard.

Coach. Look ye, Peter, it stands with reason that a conjurer should have a long grey beard—for did you ever know a witch that was not an old woman?

Gard. Why! I remember a conjurer once at a fair, that to my thinking was a very smock-fac'd man, and yet he spew'd out fifty yards of green ferret. I fancy, John, if thou'dst get him into the pantry and give him a cup of ale, he'd shew us a few tricks. Dost think we cou'd not persuade him to swallow one of thy case-knives for his diversion? he'll certainly bring it up again.

Butl. Peter, thou art such a wiseacre! thou dost not know the difference between a conjurer and a jugg'er. This man must be a very great master of his trade. His beard is at least half a yard long, he's dress'd in a strange dark cloak, as black as a coal. Your conjurer always goes in mourning.

Gard. Is he a gentleman? had he a sword by his side?

Butl. No, no, he's too grave a man for that; a conjurer is as grave as a judge—but he had a long white wand in his hand.

Coach. You may be sure there's a good deal of virtue in that wand—I fancy 'tis made out of witch-elm.

Gard. I warrant you if the ghost appears, he'll whisk ye that wand before his eyes, and strike you the drumstick out of his hand.

Butl. No: the wand, look ye, is to make a circle, and if he once gets the ghost in a circle, then he has him—let him get out again if he can. A circle, you must know, is a conjurer's trap.

Coachm. But what will he do with him, when he has him there?

Butl.

Butl. Why then he'll overpower him with his learning.

Gard. if he can once compafs him, and get him in Iob's pond, he'll make nothing of him, but fpeak a few hard words to him, and perhaps bind him over to his good be-haviour for a thoufand years.

Coachm. Ay, ay, he'll fend him packing to his grave again with a flea in his ear, I warrant him.

Butl. No, no, I would advife Madam to fpare no coft. If the conjurer be but well paid, he'll take pains upon the ghoft, and lay him, look ye, in the red-fea—and then he's laid for ever.

Coachm. Ay, marry that would fpoil his drum for him.

Gard. Why John, there muft be a power of fpirits in that fame red-fea——I warrant ye they are as plenty as fifh.

Coachm. Well, I wifh after all that he may not he too hard for the conjurer; I'm afraid he'll find a tough bit of work on't.

Gard. I wifh the fpirit may not carry a corner of the houfe off with him.

Butl. As for that, Peter, you may be fure that the Steward has made his bargain with the cunning man before hand, that he fhall ftand to all cofts and damages——but hark! yonder's Mrs Abigal, we fhall have her with us im-mediately, if we do not get off.

Gard. Ay lads! if we could get Mrs Abigal well laid too——we fhould lead merry lives.

> *For to a man like me that's ftout and bold,*
> *A ghoft is not fo dreadful as a fcold.*

ACT III.   SCENE I.

SCENE opens, and difcovers Sir George in Vellum's Office.

SIR GEORGE.

I Wonder I don't hear of Vellum yet. But I know his wifdom will do nothing rafhly. The fellow has been fo ufed to form in bufinefs, that it has infected his whole converfation. But I muft not find fault with that punc-

tual and exact behaviour, which has been of so much use
to me; my estate is the better for it.

Enter Vellum.

Well Vellum, I'm impatient to hear your success.

Vel. First, let me lock the door.

Sir Geo. Will your Lady admit me?

Vel. If this lock is not mended soon, it will be quite
spoiled.

Sir Geo. Pr'ythee let the lock alone at present, and answer me.

Vel. Delays in business are dangerous—I must send for
the Smith next week—and in the mean time will take a
minute of it.

Sir Geo. What says your Lady!

Vel. This pen is naught, and wants mending--My Lady, did you say?

Sir Geo. Does she admit me?

Vel. I have gain'd admission for you as a conjurer.

Sir Geo. That's enough! I'll gain admission for myself as a husband.   Does she believe there is any thing in
my art?

Vel. It is hard to know what a woman believes.

Sir Geo. Did she ask no questions about me!

Vel. Sundry——she desires to talk with you herself,
before you enter upon your business.

Sir Geo. But when?

Vel. Immediately.   This instant.

Sir Geo. Pugh.   What hast thou been doing all this
while! why didst not tell me so? give me my cloak——
have you yet met with Abigal?

Vel. I have not yet had an opportunity of talking with
her.   But we have interchanged some languishing glances.

Sir Geo. Let thee alone for that, Vellum, I have formerly seen thee ogle her through thy spectacles.   Well!
this is a most venerable cloak.   After the business of this
day is over, I'll make thee a present of it 'Twill become
thee mightily.

Vel. He, he, he! wou'd you make a conjurer of your
steward?

Sir Geo. Pr'ythee don't be jocular, I'm in haste.   Help
me on with my beard.

Vel.

Vel. And what will your ho nour do with your caſt beard ?

Sir Geo. Why, faith, thy gravity wants only ſuch a beard to it ; if thou would'ſt wear it with the cloak, thou would'ſt make a moſt complete heathen philoſopher. But where's my wand ?

Vel. A fine taper ſtick ! it is well choſen. I will keep this till you are ſheriff of the county. It is not my cuſtom to let any thing be loſt.

Sir Geo. Come, Vellum, lead the way. You muſt in-troduce me to your Lady. Thou'rt the fitteſt fellow in the world to be a maſter of the ceremonies to a conjurer.

[*Exeunt.*

Enter Abigal *croſſing the ſtage,* Tinſel *following.*

Tinſ. Naby, Naby, whither ſo faſt, child !

Abig. Keep your hands to yourſelf. I'm going to call the ſteward to my Lady.

Tinſ. What ? goodman twofold ? I met him walking with a ſtrange old fellow yonder. I ſuppoſe he belongs to the family too. He looks very antique. He muſt be ſome of the furniture of this old manſion houſe.

Abig. What does the man mean ? don't think to palm me, as you do my Lady.

Tinſ. Pr'ythee, Naby, tell me one thing ; what's the reaſon thou art my enemy ?

Abig. Marry, becauſe I'm a friend to my Lady.

Tinſ. Doſt thou ſee any thing about me thou doſt not like ? come hither, huſſy, give me a kiſs ; don't be ill-natur'd.

Abig Sir, I know how to be civil. [*Kiſſes her.*]——this rogue will carry off my Lady, if I don't take care.

[*aſide.*

Tinſ. Thy lips are ſoft as velvet, Abigal, I muſt get thee a huſband.

Abig. Ay, now you don't ſpeak idly, I can talk to you.

Tinſ I have one in my eye for thee. Doſt thou love a young luſty ſon of a whore ?

Abig. Laud, how you talk !

Tinſ. This is a thundering dog.

Abig. What is he !

Tinſ.

Tinſ. A private Gentleman.

Abig. Ay, where does he live ?

Tinſ. In the horſe guards——but he has one fault I moſt tell thee of. If thou canſt bear with that he's a man for thy purpoſe.

Abig. Pray, Mr Tinſel, what may that be !

Tinſ. He's but five and twenty yea s old

Abig. 'Tis no matter for his age, if he has been well educated.

Tinſ. No man better, child : he'll tye a wig, toſs a dye, make a paſs, and ſwear with ſuch a grace, as wou'd make thy heart leap to hear him.

Abig Half theſe accompliſhments will do, provided he has an eſtate—Pray what has he !

Tinſ. Not a farthing.

Abig. Pox on him, what do I give him the hearing for !   [*aſide.*

Tinſ. But as for that I wou'd make it up to him,

Abig. How ?

Tinſ. Why look ye, child, as ſoon as I have married thy Lady, I deſign to diſcard this old prig of a ſteward, and to put this honeſt gentleman, I am ſpeaking of into his place.

Abig. This fellow's a fool—I'll have no more to ſay to him. [*aſide.*]—Hark ! my Lady's a coming !

Tinſ. Depend upon it Nab, I'll remember my promiſe

Abig. Ay, and ſo will I too—to your coſt.   [*aſide.*
                                                [*Exit Abigal.*

Tinſ. My dear is purely fitted up with a maid——but I ſhall rid the houſe of her.

Enter Lady.

Lady. Oh, Mr Tinſel, I am glad to meet you here. I am going to give you an entertainment, that won't be diſagreeable to a man of wit and pleaſure of the town—— There may be ſomething diverting in a converſation between a conjurer and this conceited aſs.   [*aſide.*

Tinſ. She loves me to diſtraction, I ſee that.   [*aſide.*
—Pr'ythee, widow, explain thyſelf.

Lady.—You muſt know there is a ſtrange ſort of a man come to town, who undertakes to free the houſe from this diſturbance.   The ſteward believes him a conjurer.

Tinf. Ay; thy fteward is a deep one!

Lady. He's to be here immediately. It is indeed an odd figure of a man.

Tinf. Oh! I warrant you he has ftudy'd the black art! ha, ha, ha! is he not an Oxford fcholar?—widow, thy houfe is the moft extraordinarily inhabited of any widow's this day in Chriftendom.——I think thy four chief domefticks are—a wither'd Abigal—a fuperannuated fteward—a ghoft—and a conjurer.

Lady. [*Mimicking Tinfel.*] And you wou'd have it inhabited by a fifth, who is a more extraordinary perfon than any of all thefe four.

Tinf. It's a fure fign a woman loves you, when fhe imitates your manner. [*afide.*]—Thou'rt very fmart, my dear. But fee! fmoak the doctor.

Enter. Vellum, *and* Sir George *in his conjurer's habit.*

Vel. I will introduce this profound perfon to your Ladyfhip, and then leave him with you——Sir, this is her ho-nour.

Sir Geo. I know it well.   [*Exit Vellum.*

[*Afide, walking in a mufing pofture.*] That dear woman! the fight of her unmans me, I cou'd weep for tendernefs, did not I, at the fame time, feel an indignation rife in me, to fee that wretch with her: and yet I cannot but fmile to fee her in the company of her firft and fecond husband at the fame time.

Lady. Mr Tinfel, do you fpeak to him; you are ufed to the company of men of learning.

Tinf. Old Gentleman, thou doft not look like an inhabitant of this world; I fuppofe thou art lately come down from the ftars. Pray what news is ftirring in the zodiack?

Sir Geo. News that ought to make the heart of a coward tremble. Mars is now entring into the firft houfe, and will fhortly appear in all his domal dignities.

Tinf. Mars? Pr'ythee, father-grey-beard, explain thyfelf.

Sir Geo. The entrance of Mars into his houfe, portends the entrance of a mafter into this family—and that foon.

Tinf. D'ye hear that, widow? the ftars have cut me out for thy husband. This houfe is to have a mafter, and that

that foon—hark thee, old Gadbury, is not Mars very like a young fellow called Tom Tinfel ?

Sir Geo. Not fo much as Venus is like this Lady.

Tinf. A word in your ear, Doctor ; thefe two planets will be in conjunction by and by ; I can tell you that.

Sir Geo. [*afide, walking difturbed.*] Curfe on this impertinent fop ! I fhall fcarce forbear difcovering myfelf ——Madam, I am told that your houfe is vifited with ftrange noifes.

Lady. And I am told that you can quiet them, I muft confefs I had a curiofity to fee the perfon I had heard fo much of ; and, indeed your afpect fhows that you have had much experience in the world. You muft be a very aged man

Sir Geo My afpect deceives you ; what do you think is my real age ?

Tinf. I fhou'd guefs thee within three years of Methufelah. Pr'ythee tell me, waft thou not born before the flood ?

Lady. Truly I fhou'd guefs you to be in your fecond or third century. I warrant you, you have great grandchildren with beards of a foot long.

Sir Geo. Ha, ha, ha ! if there be truth in man. I was but five and thirty laft Auguft. O ! the ftudy of the occult fciences makes a man's beard grow fafter than you would imagine.

Lady. What an efcape you have had, Mr Tinfel, that you were not bred a fcholar !

Tinf. And fo I fancy, doctor, thou think'ft me an illiterate fellow, becaufe I have a fmooth chin ?

Sir Geo. Hark ye, Sir, a word in your ear. You are a coxcomb by all the rules of phyfiognomy : but let that be a fecret between you and me.   {*afide to Tinfel.*

Lady. Pray, Mr Tinfel, what is it the doctor whifpers ?

Tinf. Only a compliment, child, upon two or three of my features. It does not become me to repeat it.

Lady Pray, doctor, examine this Gentleman's face, and tell me his fortune.

Sir Geo. If I may believe the lines of his face, he likes it better than I do, or——than you do, fair Lady.

Tinf. Widow, I hope now thou'rt convinc'd he's a cheat,

Lady.

Lady. For my part I believe he's a witch——go on, ·doctor.

Sir Geo. He will be crofs'd in love; and that foon.

Tinf. Pr'ythee, doctor, tell us the truth. Doft not thou live in Moor-fields?

Sir Geo. Take my word for it, thou fhalt never live in my Lady Trueman's manfion-houfe.

Tinf. Pray, old Gentleman, haft thou never been pluck-ed by the beard when thou wert faucy?

Lady. Nay, Mr Tinfel, you are angry! do thou think I wou'd marry a man that dares not have his fortune told?

Sir Geo. Let him be angry——I matter not——he is but fhort liv'd. He will foon die of——

Tinf. Come, come, fpeak out, old Hocus, he, he, he! this fellow makes me burft with laughing. [*Forces a laugh.*

Sir Geo. He will foon die of a fright——or of the—let me fee your nofe—— ay——'tis fo!

Tinf. You fon of a whore! I'll run you through the body. I never yet made the fun fhine through a conju-rer.

Lady. Oh, fy, Mr Tinfel! you will not kill an old man?

Tinf. An old man! the dog fays he's but five and thirty.

Lady. Oh, fy, Mr Tinfel, I did not think you could have been fo paffionate; I hate a paffionate man. Put up your fword, or I muft never fee you again.

Tinf. Ha, ha, ha! I was but in jeft, my dear. I had a mind to have made an experiment upon the doctor's body. I wou'd have but drill'd a little eye-let hole in it, and have feen whether he had art enough no clofe it up again.

Sir Geo. Courage is but ill fhown before a Lady. But know, if ever I meet thee again thou fhalt find this arm can wield other weapons befides this wand.

Tinf. Ha, ha, ha!

Lady. Well, learned Sir, you are to give a proof of your art, not of your courage. Or if you will fhow your courage, let it be at nine o'clock——for that is the time the noife is generally heard.

Tinf. And look, ye, old Gentleman, if thou doft not do thy bufinefs well, I can tell thee by the little fkill I

have,

have, that thou wilt be tofs'd in a blanket before ten.
We'll do our endeavour to fend thee back to the ftars
again.

Sir Geo. I'll go and prepare myfelf for the ceremonies——and Lady, as you expect they fhou'd fucceed to
your wifhes, treat that fellow with the contempt he de-
ferves.   [*Exit* Sir George.

Tinf. The fauciest dog I ever talk'd with in my whole
life *!*

Lady. Methinks he's a diverting fellow ;   may fee
he's no fool.   one

Tinf. No fool ! ay, but thou doft not take him for a
conjurer.

Lady. Truly I don't know what to take him for ; I
am refolv'd to employ him however. When a ficknefs
is defperate, we often try remedies that we have no
great faith in.

Enter Abigal.

Abig. Madam, the tea is ready in the parlour, as you
order'd.

Lady. Come, Mr Tinfel, we may there talk of this
fubject more at leifure.   [*Exeunt Lady and Tinfel.*

Abigal *fola.*

Sure never any Lady had fuch fervants as mine has !
well, if I get this thoufand pounds, I hope to have fome
of my own. Let me fee, I'll have a pretty tight girl—
juft fuch as I was ten years ago (I'm afraid I may fay
twenty) fhe fhall drefs me and flatter me——for I
will be flatter'd, that's pos ! my Lady's caft fuits will
ferve her, after I have given them the wearing. Befides, when I am worth a thoufand pounds, I fhall, certainly carry off the fteward——Madam Vellum——
how prettily that will found ! here, bring out Madam Vellum's chaife——nay, I do not know but it may be a cha-
riot——It will break the attorney's wife's heart——for
I fhall take place of every body in the parifh but my
Lady. If I have a fon, he fhall be call'd Fantome. But
fee Mr Vellum, as I could wifh. I know his humour,
and I will do my utmoft to gain his heart.

Enter Vellum *with a pint of Sack.*

Vel. Mrs Abigal, don't I break in upon you unfea-
fonably ?

                                                        Abig.

Abig. Oh, no, Mr Vellum, your visits are always sea-sonable.

Vel. I have brought with me a taste of fresh Canary, which I think is delicious.

Abig. Pray set it down—I have a dram glass just by—
[*Brings in a Rummer.*
I'll pledge you ; my Lady's good health.

Vel. and your own with it———sweet Mrs Abigal.

Abig Pray, good Mr Vellum, buy me a little parcel of this sack, and put it under the article of tea———I would not have my name appear to it.

Vel. Mrs Abigal, your name seldom appears in my bills———and———yet if you will allow me a merry expression———you have been always in my books, Mrs Abigal, Ha, ha, ha !

Abig. Ha, ha, ha ! Mr Vellum, you are such a dry jesting man.

Vel. Why truly, Mrs Abigal, I have been looking over my papers------and I find you have been a long time my debtor.

Abig. Your debtor for what, Mr Vellum?

Vel. For my heart, Mrs Abigal, and our accounts will not be ballanc'd between us, till I have yours in exchange for it, Ha, ha, ha !

Abig. Ha, ha, ha ! you are the most gallant dun, Mr Vellum.

Vel. But I am not us'd to be paid by words only, Mrs Abigal ; when will you be out of my debt ?

Abig. Oh, Mr Vellum, you make one blush—my humble service to you.

Vel. I must answer you, Mrs Abigal, in the country phrase—*Your love is sufficient.* Ha, ha, ha !

Abig. Ha, ha, ha ! Well, I must own, I love a merry man !

Vel. Let me see, how long is it, Mrs Abigal, since I first broke my mind to you—it was, I think, *Undecimo Gulielmi,*------we have conversed together these fifteen years—and yet, Mrs Abigal, I must drink to our better acquaintance. He, he, he,—Mrs Abigal, you know I am naturally jocose.

Abig.

D

Abig Ah, you men love to make fport with us filly creatures.

Vel. Mrs Abigal, I have a trifle about me, which I would willingly make you a prefent of. It is indeed but a little toy.

Abig. You are always exceedingly obliging.

Vel. It is but a little toy ——fcarce worth your acceptance.

Abig. Pray don't keep me in fufpence; what is it, Mr Vellum?

Vel. A filver thimble.

Abig. I always faid Mr Vellum was a generous lover.

Vel. But I mult put it on myfelf, Mrs Abigal,—you have the prettieft tip of a finger.——I mult take the freedom to falute it.

Abig. Oh fy! you make me afham'd, Mr Vellum; how can you do fo? I proteft I am in fuch a confufion—

A feigned ftruggle.

Vel. This finger is not the finger of idlenefs; it bears the honourable fcars of the needle— but why are you fo cruel as not to pare your nails?

Abig. Oh, I vow you prefs it fo hard! pray give me my finger again.

Vel. This middle finger, Mrs Abigal, has a pretty neighbour— a wedding-ring would become it mightily.·· He, he, he!

Abig. You're fo full of your jokes. Ay, but where mult I find one for it?

Vel. I defign this thimble only as the forerunner of it. They will fet off each other, and are···indeed a twofold emblem. The fult will put you in mind of being a good houfe wife, and the other of being a good wife. Ha, ha, I·!

Abig. Yes, yes, I fee you laugh at me.

Vel. Indeed I am ferious.

Abig. I thought you had quite forfaken me········I am fure you cannot forget the many repeated vows and promifes you formerly made me.

Vel. I fhould as foon forget the multiplication table.

Abig I have always taken your part before my Lady.

Vel. You have fo, and I have *item'd* it in my memory.

Abig.

Abig. For I have always look'd upon your interests as my own.

Vel. It is nothing but your cruelty can hinder them from being so.

Abig. I must strike while the iron's hot. [*Aside.*]— Well, Mr Vellum, there's no refusing you, you have such a bewitching tongue!

Vel. How? speak that again!

Abig. Why then in plain English I love you.

Vel. I'm overjoy'd!

Abig. I must own my passion for you.

Vel. I'm transported! *Catches her in his arms.*

Abig. Dear charming man!

Vel. Thou sum total of all my happiness!---I shall grow extravagant! I can't forbear to drink thy virtuous incli‑ nations in a bumper of Sack. Your Lady must make haste, my duck, or we shall provide a young steward to the estate, before she has an heir to it ---Pr'ythee, my dear, does she intend to marry Mr Tinsel?

Abig. Marry him, my love, no, no! we must take care of that! there would be no staying in the house for us if she did. That young Rake-hell would send all the old servants a-grazing. You and I should be discarded before the honey moon was at an end.

Vel. Pr'ythee, sweet one, does not this drum put the thoughts of marriage out of her head?

Abig. This drum, my dear, if it be well manag'd, will be no less than a thousand pound in our way.

Vel. Ay, say'st thou so, my turtle?

Abig. Since we are now as good as man and wife-- I I mean, almost as good as man and wife---I ought to con‑ ceal nothing from you.

Vel. Certainly, my dove, not from thy yoke-fellow, thy help-mate, thy own flesh and blood!

Abig. Hush! I hear Mr Tinsel's laugh, my Lady and he are coming this way; if you will take a turn without I'll tell you the whole contrivance.

Vel. Give me your hand, chicken.

Abig. Here take it, you have my heart already.

Vel. We shall have much issue. [*Exeunt.*

ACT

ACT IV.   SCENE I.

Enter Vellum *and* Butler.

VELLUM.

JOHN, I have certain orders to give you---and therefore be attentive.

Butl. Attentive! Ay, let me alone for that-- I suppose
he means being sober.   [*Aside.*

Vel. You know I have always recommended to you a
method in your business: I wou'd have your knives and
forks, your spoons and napkins, your plate and glasses,
laid in a method.

Butl. Ah, Mr Vellum, you are such a sweet spoken
man it does one's heart good to receive your orders.

Vel. Method, John, makes business easy, it banishes all
perplexity and confusion out of families.

Butl. How he talks! I could hear him all day.

Vel. And now, John, let me know whether your table-
linen, your side board, your cellar, and every thing else
within your province, are properly and methodically dis-
pos'd for an entertainment this evening.

Butl. Master Vellum, they shall be ready at a quarter
of an hour's warning. But pray Sir, is this entertainment
to be made for the conjurer?

Vel. It is, John, for the conjurer, and yet it is not
for the conjurer.

Butl. Why, look you Master Vellum, if it is for the
conjurer, the cook maid shou'd have orders to get him
some dishes to his palate. Perhaps he may like a little
brimstone in his sauce.

Vel. This conjurer, John, is a complicated creature,
an amphibious animal, a person of a twofold nature----,
but he eats and drinks like other men.

Butl. Marry, Master Vellum, he shou'd eat and drink
as much as two other men, by the account you give of
him.

Vel. Thy conceit is not amis's, he is indeed a double
man, ha, ha, ha!

                                        Butl.

Butl. Ha ! I underſtand you, he's one of your herma-phrodites, as they call 'em.

Vel. He is married, and he is not married---he hath a beard, and he hath no beard. He is old, and he is young.

Butl. How charmingly he talks ! I fancy, Maſter Vel-lum, you could make a riddle. The ſame man old and young ! how do you make that out, Maſter Vellum ?

Vel. Thou haſt heard of a ſnake caſting his ſkin, and recovering his youth. Such is this ſage perſon.

Butl. Nay, 'tis no wonder a conjurer ſhould be like a ſerpent.

Vel. When he has thrown aſide the old conjurer's ſlough that hangs about him, he'll come out as fine a young gentleman as ever was ſeen in this houſe.

Butl. Does he intend to ſup in his ſlough ?

Vel. That time will ſhow.

Butl. Well. I have not a head for theſe things. Indeed, Mr Vellum I have not underſtood one word you have ſaid this half hour.

Vel. I did not intend thou ſhou'dſt—but to our buſi-neſs—let there be a table ſpread in the great hall. Let your pots and glaſſes be waſh'd, and in a readineſs. Bid the cook provide a plentiful ſupper, and ſee that all the ſervants be in their beſt liveries.

Butl. Ay ! now I underſtand every word you ſay, But I wou'd rather hear you talk a little in that t'other way.

Vel. I ſhall explain to thee what I have ſaid by and by ——— bid Suſan lay two pillows upon your Lady's bed.

Butl. Two, pillows ! Madam won't ſleep upon 'em both ! ſhe is not a double woman too.

Vel. She will ſleep upon neither But hark, Mrs Abi-ga', I think I hear her chiding the cook maid.

Butl. Then I'll away, or it will be my turn next; ſhe, I am ſure ſpeaks plain Engliſh, one may eaſily underſtand every word ſhe ſays. [*Exit Butler.*

Vellum *ſolus.*

Vel. Servants are good for nothing, unleſs they have an opinion of the perſon's underſtanding who has the direc-tion of them—but ſee Mrs Abigal ! ſhe has a bewitching countenance,

countenance, I wish I may not be tempted to marry her in good earneft.

Enter Abigal.

Abig. Ha! Mr Vellum.

Vel. What brings my fweet one-hither?

Abig. I am coming to fpeak to my friend behind the wainfcot. It is fit, child, he fhould have an account of this conjurer, that he may not be furpris'd.

Vel. That wou'd be as much as thy thoufand pound is worth.

Abig. I'll fpeak low—wall's have ears.

[*Pointing at the wainfcot.*

Vel. But hark you, ducklin! be fure you do not tell h'm that I am let into the fecret.

Abig. That's a good one indeed! as if I fhould ever tell what paffes between you and me.

Vel. No, no, my child, that muft not be, he, he, he! that muft not be: he, he, he!

Abig. You will always be waggifh.

Vel. Adieu, and let me hear the refult of your confe-rence.

Abig How can you leave one fo foon? I fhall think it an age till I fee you again.

Vel. Adieu my pretty one.

Abig. Adieu fweet Mr Vellum!

Vel. My pretty one——   [*As he is going off.*

Abig. Dear Mr Vellum!

Vel. My pretty one!   [*Exit* Vellum.

Abigal *fola.*

Abig. I have him——If I can but get this thoufand pound.   [*Fantome gives three raps upon his drum behind the wainfcot.*

Abig. Ha! three raps upon the drum! the fignal Mr Fantome and I agreed upon, when he had a mind to fpeak with me.   [*Fantome raps again.*

Abig. Very well, I hear you; come fox, come out of your hole.

Scene opens, and Fantome comes out.

Abig. You may leave your drum in the wardrobe, till you have occafion for it.

Fan:

Fant. Well, Mrs Abigal, I want to hear what is a do-ing in the world.

Abig. You are a very inquiſitive ſpirit. But I muſt tell you, if you do not take care of yourſelf, you will be laid this evening.

Fant. I have overheard ſomething of that matter. But let me alone for the doſtor——I'll engage to give a good account of him. I am more in pain about Tinſel. When a Lady's in the caſe, I'm more afraid of one fop than twenty conjurers.

Abig. To tell you truly, he preſſes his attacks with ſo much impudence, that he has made more progreſs with my Lady in two days, than you did in two months.

Fant. I ſhall attack her in another manner, if thou canſt but procure me another interview. There's nothing makes a lover ſo keen, as being kept up in the dark.

Abig. Pray no more of your diſtant bows, your reſpect-ful compliments——really, Mr Fantome, you're only fit to make love a croſs a tea-table.

Fant. My dear girl, I can't forbear hugging thee for thy good advice.

Abig. Ay, now I have ſome hopes of you; but why don't you do ſo to my Lady?

Fant. Child, I always thought your Lady lov'd to be treated with reſpect.

Abig. Believe me, Mr Fantome, there is not ſo great a difference between woman and woman, as you imagine. You ſee Tinſel has nothing but his ſauucineſs to recom-mend him.

Fant. Tinſel is too great a coxcomb to be capable of love—and let me tell thee, Abigal, a man, who is ſincere in his paſſion, makes but a very aukward profeſſion of it ——but I'll mend my manners.

Abig. Ay, or you'll never gain a widow—come, I muſt tutor you a little; ſuppoſe me to be my Lady, and let me ſee how you'll behave yourſelf.

Fant. I'm afraid, child, we han't time for ſuch a piece of mummery.

Abig. Oh, 'twill be quickly over, if you play your part well.

Fant.

Fant. Why then, dear Mrs Ab——I mean my Lady Trueman.

Abig. Ay! but you han't faluted me.

Fant That's right; faith I forgot that circumstance, [*Kiffes her.*] Nectar and Ambrosia!

Abig. That's very well——

Fant. How long must I be condemned to languish! when shall my fufferings have an end! my life! my happinefs, my all is wound up in you ——

Abig. Well! why don't you fqueeze my hand?

Fant. What, thus!

Abig. Thus? ay—now throw your arm about my middle; hug me clofer——you are not afraid of hurting me! now pour forth a volley of rapture and nonfenfe, till you are out of breath.

Fant. Tranfport and extacy! Where am I——my life, my blefs! I rage, I burn, I bleed, I die!

Abig. Go on, go on.

Fant. Flames and darts—bear me to the gloomy fhade, rocks and grottos—flowers, zephyrs, and purling ftreams.

Abig. Oh Mr Fantome, you have a tongue would undo a veftal! you were born for the ruin of our fex.

Fant. This will do then, Abigal?

Abig Ay, this is talking like a lover. Tho' I only reprefent my Lady, I take a pleafure in hearing you. Well, o' my con'cience when a man of fenfe has a little dafh of the coxcomb in him, no woman can refift him. Go on at this rate, and the thoufand pound is as good as in my pocket.

Fant. I fhall think it an age till I have an opportunity of putting this leffon in practice.

Abig You may do it foon, if you make good ufe of your time; Mr Tinfel will be here with my Lady at eight, and at nine the conjurer is to take you in hand.

Fant. Let me alone with them both

Abig. Well! forewarn'd, forearm'd. Get into your box, and I'll endeavour to difpofe every thing in your favour.   [*Fantome goes in. Exit Abigal.*
Enter Vellum

Vel. Mrs Abigal is withdrawn ——I was in hopes to have heard what had pafs'd between her and her invifible correfpondent.

Tinf.

Enter Tinsel.

Tinf. Vellum! Vellum!

Vel. Vellum! we are methinks very familiar; I am
not us'd to be called so by any but their ho-nours [*aside.*]
—What wou'd you, Mr Tinsel!

Tinf. Let me beg a favour of thee, old Gentleman.

Vel. What is that, good Sir?

Tinf. Pr'ythee-run and fetch me the rent-roll of thy
Lady's estate.

Vel. The rent roll!

Tinf The rent-roll? ay, the rent-roll! dost not understand what that means?

Vel. Why? have you any thoughts of purchasing of it?

Tinf. Thou hast hit it, old boy, that is my very in-
tention.

Vel. The purchase will be considerable.

Tinf. And for that reason I have bid thy Lady very
high——she is to have no less for it than this intire person of mine.

Vel. Is your whole estate personal, Mr Tinsel!——
he, he, he!

Tinf. Why, you queer old dog, you don't pretend to
jest, d'ye! look ye, Vellum, if you think of being con-
tinued my steward, you must learn to walk with your
toes out.

Vel. An insolent companion!   [*aside*

Tinf. Thou'rt confounded rich I see, by that dangling
of thy arms.

Vel. An ungracious bird!   [*aside.*

Tinf. Thou shalt lend me a couple of thousand pounds.

Vel. A very profligate!   [*aside.*

Tinf. Look ye, Vellum, I intend to be kind to you—
I'll borrow some money of you.

Vel. I cannot but smile to consider the disappointment
this young fellow will meet with; I will make myself
merry with him [*aside.*]—and so, Mr Tinsel, you pro-
mise you will be a very kind master to me? [*stifling a
laugh.*

Tinf. What will you give for a life in the house you
live in?

V^{le}

Vel. What do you think of five hundred pounds? ha, ha, ha!

Tinf. That's too little.

Vel. And yet it is more than I shall give——and I will offer you two reasons for it.

Tinf. Pr'ythee what are they!

Vel. First, because the tenement in not in your difpofal; and secondly, because it never will be in your difpofal; and so fare you well, good Mr Tinfel. Ha, ha, ha! you will pardon me for being jocular.   [*Exit* Vellum.

Tinf. This rogue is as fawcy as the conjurer; I'll be hang'd if they are not a kin.

Enter Lady.

Lady. Mr Tinfel! what, all alone? you freethinkers are great admirers of solitude.

Tinf. No faith, I have been talking with thy steward; a very grotesque figure of a fellow, the very picture of one of our benchers. How can you bear his conversation?

Lady. I keep him for my steward, and not my companion. He's a sober man.

Tinf. Yes, yes, he looks like a put——a queer old dog, as ever I faw in my life: we must turn him off, widow. He cheats thee confoundedly, I see that.

Lady. Indeed you're miftaken, he has always had the reputation of being a very honest man.

Tinf. What, I suppofe he goes to church.

Lady Goes to church! so do you too, I hope.

Tinf. I wou'd for once, widow, to make sure of you.

Lady. Ah, Mr Tinfel, a husband who would not continue to go thither, would quickly forget the promises he made there.

Tinf. Faith very innocent and very ridiculous! well then, I warrant thee, widow, thou wou'dft not for the world marry a sabbath breaker!

Lady. Truly they generally come to a bad end. I remember the conjurer told you, you were short-liv'd.

Tinf. The conjurer, ha, ha, ha!

Lady. indeed you're very witty!

Tinf. Indeed you're very handfome. [*Kiffes her hand.*

Lady. I wifh the fool does not love me!   [*afide.*

Tinf. Thou art the idol I adore. Here muft I pay my
devotion

devotion———Pr'ythee, widow, haſt thou any timber upon thy eſtate?

Lady. The moſt impudent fellow I ever met with.

                          [*aſide.*

Tinſ. I take notice thou haſt a great deal of old plate here in the houſe, widow.

Lady. Mr Tinſel. you are a very obſerving man.

Tinſ. Thy large ſilver ciſtern would make a very good coach ; and half a dozen ſalvers that I ſaw on the ſideboard, might be turned into ſix as pretty horſes as any that appear in the ring.

Lady. You have a very good fancy, Mr Tinſel—— what pretty transformations you cou'd make in my houſe —but I'll ſee where 'twill end.   [*aſide.*

Tinſ. Then I obſerve, child, you have two or three ſervices of gilt plate ; we'd eat always in china, my dear.

Lady. I perceive you are an excellent manager—how quickly you have taken an inventory of my goods !

Tinſ. Now hark ye, widow, to ſhow you the love that I have for you——

Lady. Very well, let me hear.

Tinſ. You have an old faſhion'd gold caudle-cup, with the figure of a ſaint upon the lid on't.

Lady I have : what then?

Tinſ. Why look ye, I'd ſell the caudle-cup, with the old ſaint, for as much money as they'd fetch, which I wou'd convert into a diamond buckle, and make you a preſent of it.

Lady. Oh you are generous to an extravagance. But pray, Mr Tinſel, don't diſpoſe of my goods before you are ſure of my perſon. I find you have taken a great affection to my moveables.

Tinſ. My dear I love every thing that belongs to you.

Lady. I ſee you do, Sir, you need not make any proteſtations upon that ſubject.

Tinſ. Pho, pho, my dear, we are growing ſerious, and let me tell you, that's the very next ſtep to being dull. Come, that pretty face was never made to look grave with.

Lady. Believe me Sir, whatever you may think, marriage is a ſerious ſubject.

Tinſ. For that very reaſon, my dear, let us get over it as faſt as we can.

                                     Lady.

Lady. I should be very much in haste for a husband, if I married within fourteen months after Sir George's deceafe.

Tinf. Pray my dear, let me ask you a queflion ; do'st not thou think that Sir George is as dead at prefent, to all intents and purpofes, as he will be a twelve month hence ?

Lady. Yes, but decency, Mr Tinfel!————

Tinf. Or doft thou think thou'lt be more a widow than thou art now ?

Lady. The world, would fay I never lov'd my firft hufband.

Tinf. Ah, my dear, they would fay you lov'd your fecond ; and they wou'd own I deferv'd it, for I fhall love thee moft inordinately.

Lady. But what wou'd people think ?

Tinf. Think ! why they wou'd think thee the mirrour of widowhood——That a woman fhou'd live fourteen whole months after the deceafe of her fpoufe, without having engaged herfelf. Why, about town, we know many a woman of quality's fecond hufband feveral years before the death of the firft.

Lady. Ay, I know you wits have your common——place jefts upon us poor widows.

Tinf. I'll tell you a flory, widow; I know a certain Lady, who, confidering the crazinefs of her husband, had, in cafe of mortality, engaged herfelf to two young fellows of my acquaintance. They grew fuch defperate riva's for her while her husband was alive, that one of them pink'd the t'other in a duel But the good Lady was no fooner a widow, but what did my dowager do ? wh faith, being a woman of honour, fhe married a third, to whom, it feems, fhe had given her firft promife.

Lady. And this is a true ftory upon your own knowledge ?

Tinf Every tittle, as I hope to be marry'd, or never believe Tom Tinfel.

Lady. Pray, Mr Tinfel, do you call this talking like a wit, or like a rake ?

Tinf.

Tinf. Innocent enough, he, he, he ! why where's the difference, my dear ?

Lady. Yes, Mr Tinfel, the only man I ever lov'd in my life, had a great deal of the one, and nothing of the other in him.

Tinf. Nay, now you grow vapourish ; thou'lt begin to fancy thou hear'ft the drum by and by.

Lady. If you had been here laft night about this time, you wou'd not ha'c been fo merry.

Tinf. About this time, fay'ft thou ? come faith, for the humour's fake, we'll fit down and liften.

Lady. I will, if you'll promife to be feriou°.

Tinf. Serious ! never fear me, child. Ha, ha, ha ! do'ft not hear him ?

Lady. You break your word already. Pray, Mr Tin-fel, do you laugh to fhow your wit or your teeth ?

Tinf. Why, both ! my dear—— I'm glad however, that fhe has taken notice of my teeth. [*afide*] But you look ferious, child ? I fancy thou hear'ft the drum, do'ft not ?

Lady. Don't talk fo rafhly.

Tinf. Why, my dear, you cou'd not look more fright-ed if you had Lucifer's drum-major in your houfe.

Lady. Mr Tinfel, I muft defire to fee you no more in it, if you do not leave this idle way of talking.

Tinf. Child, I thought I had told you what is my opi-nion of fpirits, as we were drinking a difh of tea but juft now———There is no fuch thing, I give thee my word.

Lady. Oh, Mr Tinfel, your authority muft be of great weight to thofe that know you.

Tinf. For my part, child, I have made myfelf eafy in thofe points.

Lady. Sure nothing was ever like this fellow's vanity, but his ignorance. [*afide.*

Tinf. I'll tell thee what now, widow——I wou'd en-gage by the help of a white fheet and a penny-worth of link in a dark night, to frighten you a whole courtry vil-lage out of their fenfes, and the vicar into the bargain. [*drum beats.*] Hark ! hark ! what noife is that ! hea-ven defend us ! this is more than fancy.

Lady.

Lady It beats more terrible than ever .

Tinf. 'Tis very dreadful? what a dog have I been to speak against my conscience, only to show my parts !

Lady. It comes nearer and nearer. I wish you have not anger'd it by your foolish discourse.

Tinf. Indeed, Madam, I did not speak from my heart ; I hope it will do me no hurt for a little harmless raillery.

Lady. Harmless, d'ye call it? it beats hard by us, as if it wou'd break through the wall.

Tinf. What a devil had I to do with a white sheet ?
                    [*Scene opens, and discovers Fantome.*

Tinf. Mercy on us ! it appears.

Lady Oh ! 'tis he ! 'tis he himself, 'tis Sir George ! 'tis my husband !   [*She faints.*

Tinf. Now wou'd I give ten thousand pound that I were in town.   [*Fantome advances to him drumming.* I beg ten thousand pardons   I'll never talk at this rate any more.   [*Fantome still advances drumming.*

By my soul, Sir George, I was not in earnest (*Falls on his knees*) have compassion on my youth, and consider I am but a coxcomb——(*Fantome points to the door*) But see he waves me off——ay, with all my heart——What a devil had I to do with a white sheet ?

(*He steals off the stage, mending his pace as the drum beats.*

Fant. The scoundrel is gone, and has left his mistress behind him. I'm mistaken if he makes love in this house any more. I have now only the conjurer to deal with. I don't question but I shall make his reverence scamper as fast as the lover. And then the day's my own. But the servants are coming, I must get into my cup-board.
                         (*He goes in.*

Enter Abigal *and servants.*

Abig. O my poor Lady ! this wicked drum has frighted Mr Tinsel out of his wits, and my Lady into a swoon. Let me bend her a little forward. She revives Here, carry her into the fresh air, and she'll recover. (*They carry her off*) This is a little barbarous to my Lady, but 'tis all for her good : and I know her so well, that she wou'd not be angry with me, if she knew what I was to get by it. And if any other friends shou'd blame me for it hereafter,

I'll

I'll clap my hand upon my purse, and tell 'em,
'Twas for a thousand pound, and Mr Vellum.

ACT V.   SCENE I.

Enter Sir George in his conjurer's habit, the Butler
marching before him with two large candles, and the
two servants coming after him; one bringing a little
table, and another a chair.

BUTLER.

AN'T please your worship, Mr Conjurer, the Steward has given all of us orders to do whatsoever you shall bid us, and to pay you the same respect, as if you were our master.

Sir Geo. Thou say'st well.

Gard. An't please you Conjurership's worship, shall I set the table down here?

Sir Geo. Here, Peter.

Gard. Peter!——he knows my name by his learning.
[*aside.*

Coachm. I have brought you, reverend Sir, the largest elbow-chair in the house; 'tis that the Steward sits in when he holds a court.

Sir Geo. Place it there.

Butl. Sir, will you please to want any thing else?

Sir Geo. Paper, and a pen and ink.

Butl. Sir, I believe we have paper that is fit for your purpose! my Lady's mourning paper, that is black'd at the edges—wou'd you chuse to write with a crow quill?

Sir Geo. There is none better.

Butl. Coachman, go fetch the paper and standish out of the little parlour.

Coachm. [*to the Gardiner.*] Peter, pr'ythee do you go along with me——I'm afraid——you know I went with you last night into the garden, when the cook maid wanted a handful of parsley.

Butl. Why, you don't think I'll stay with the Conjurer by myself?

Gard.

E 2

Gard. Come we'll all three go and fetch the pen and ink together.   *(Exeunt Servants.*
                    Sir George *solus.*

There's nothing, I fee, makes fuch ftrong alliances as fear. Thefe fellows are all enter'd into a confederacy againft the Ghoft. There muft be abundance of bufinefs done in the family at this rate. But here comes the triple alliance. Who cou'd have thought thefe three rogues cou'd have found each of 'em an employment in fetching a pen and ink !

Enter Gardiner *with a fheet of paper,* Coachman *with a ftandifh, and* Butler *with a pen.*

Gard. Sir, there is your paper.

Coachm. Sir, there is your ftandifh.

Butl. Sir, there is your crow-quill pen————I'm glad I have got rid on't.   *(afide.*

Gard. He forgets that he's to make a circle.   *(afide.*
————Doctor, fhall I help you to a bit of chalk ?

Sir Geo. It is no matter.

Butl Look ye, Sir, I fhow'd you the fpot where he's heard ofteneft, if your worfhip can but ferret him out of that old wall in that next room————

Sir Geo. We fhall try.

Gard. That's right, John. His worfhip muft let fly all his learning at that old wall.

Butl. Sir, if I was worthy to advife you, I wou'd have a bottle of good October by me. Shall I fet a cup of old ftingo at your elbow ?

Sir Geo. I thank thee, we fhall do without it.

Gard. John, he feems a very good natur'd man for a conjurer.

Butl. I'll take this opportunity of enquiring after a bit of plate I have loft. I fancy, whilft he is in my Lady's pay, one may hedge in a queftion or two into the bargain. Sir, Sir, may I beg a word in your ear ?

Sir Geo. What wouldft thou ?

Butl Sir, I know I need not tell you, that I loft one of my filver fpoons laft week.

Sir Geo. Mark'd with a fwan's neck————

Butl. My Lady's Creft ! He knows every thing. *(afide.)* How wou'd your worfhip advife me to recover it again ?

                                        Sir Geo.

Sir Geo. Hum !

Butl. What muſt I do to come at it ?

Sir Geo. Drink nothing but ſmall beer for a fort-night——

Butl. Small-beer ! rot gut !

Sir Geo. If thou drink'ſt a ſingle drop of ale before fifteen days are expir'd——it is as much——as thy ſpoon——is worth.

Butl. I ſhall never recover it that way ; I'll e'en buy a new one.

Coachm. D'ye mind how they whiſper ?

Gard. I'll be hang'd if he be not asking him ſomething about Nell——

Coachm. I'll take this opportunity of putting a queſtion to him about poor Dobbin : I fancy he cou'd give me better counſel than the farrier.

Butl. [*to the Gardiner.*] A prodigious man ! he knows every thing : now is the time to find out thy pick-ax.

Gard. I have nothing to give him . does not he expect to have his hand croſs'd with ſilver ?

Coachm. [*to Sir George.*] Sir, may a man venture to ask you a queſtion.

Sir Geo. Ask it.

Coachm. I have a poor horſe in the ſtable that's be-witch'd——

Sir Geo. A bay gelding.

Coachm. How cou'd he know that ?—— [*aſide.*

Sir Geo. Bought at Banbury.

Coachm. Whew—ſo it was o' my conſcience. [*Whiſtles.*

Sir Geo. Six years old laſt Lammas.

Coachm. To a day. [*Aſide.*] Now, Sir, I wou'd know whether the poor beaſt is bewitch'd by Goody Crouch or Goody Flye ?

Sir Geo. Neither.

Coachm. Then it muſt be Goody Gurton ! for ſhe is next oldeſt woman in the pariſh.

Gard. Haſt thou done, Robin ?

Coachm. [*to the Gardiner.*] He can tell thee any thing.

Gard. [*to Sir George.*] Sir, I would beg to take you a little further out of hearing——

Sir Geo. Speak.

Gard.

Gard. The butler and I, Mr Doctor, were both of us in love at the same time with a certain person.

Sir Geo. A woman.

Gard. How could he know that?   [*Aside.*

Sir Geo. Go on.

Gard. This woman has lately had two children at a birth.

Sir Geo. Twins.

Gard. Prodigious! where could he hear that. [*Aside.*

Sir Geo. Proceed.

Gard. Now because I us'd to meet her sometimes in the garden, she has laid them both——

Sir Geo. To thee.

Gard. What a power of learning he must have; he knows ev'ry thing.   [*aside.*

Sir Geo. Hast thou done?

Gard. I wou'd desire to know whether I am really father to them both?

Sir Geo. Stand before me, let me survey thee round.
            [*Lays his wand upon his head, and makes him turn about.*

Coachm. Look yonder, John, the silly dog is turning about under the conjurer's wand. If he has been saucy to him, we shall see him puff'd off in a whirlwind immediately.

Sir Geo. Twins, do'st thou say! [*Still turning him.*

Gard. Ay; are they both mine d'ye think?

Sir Geo. Own but one of them.

Gard. Ah! but Mrs Abigal will have me take care of them both—she's always for the butler—if my poor master Sir George had been alive, he would have made him go halves with me.

Sir Geo. What, was Sir George a kind master!

Gard. Was he! ay, my fellow-servants will bear me witness.

Sir Geo. Did you love Sir George?

Butl. Every body lov'd him——

Coachm. There was not a dry eye in the parish at the news of his death——

Gard. He was the best neighbour——

Butl. The kindest husband ——

                                        _ *Coachm.*

Coachm. The trueſt friend to the poor——

Butl. My good Lady took on mightily, we all thought
it would have been the death of her.

Sir Geo. I proteſt theſe fellows melt me! I think the
time long till I am their maſter again, that I may be kind
to them. [*aſide.*

Enter Vellum.

Vel. Have you provided the doctor ev'ry thing he had
occaſion for ? if ſo—you may depart. [*Exeunt Servants.*

Sir Geo. I can as yet ſee no hurt in my wife's behaviour ; but ſtill have ſome certain pangs and doubts, that
are natural to the heart of a fond man. I muſt take
the advantage of my diſguiſe to be thoroughly ſatisfied.
It would neither be for her happineſs, nor mine to make
myſelf known to her till I am ſo. [*aſide.*]—Dear Vellum, I am impatient to hear ſome news of my wife, how
does ſhe after her fright ?

Vel. It is a ſaying ſomewhere in my Lord Coke, that
a widow——

Sir Geo. I ask of my wife, and thou talk'ſt to me of
my Lord Coke—Pr'ythee tell me how ſhe does, for I
am in pain for her,

Vel. She is pretty well recover'd. Mrs Abigal has
put her in good heart ; and I have given her great hopes
from your skill.

Sir Geo. That I think cannot fail, ſince thou haſt got
this ſecret out of Abigal. But I could not have thought
my friend Fantome would have ſerv'd me thus—

Vel. You will ſtill fancy you are a living man—

Sir Geo. That he ſhould endeavour to enſnare my
wife.

Vel. You have no right in her, after your demiſe :
death extinguiſhes all property,——*Quod hanc*—it is a
maxim in the law.

Sir Geo. A pox on your learning ! well, but what is
become of Tinſel ?

Vel. He ruſh'd out of the houſe, call'd for his horſe,
clap'd ſpurs to his ſides, and was out of ſight in leſs time
than I can—tel—ten.

Sir Geo. This is whimſical enough ! my wife will
have a quick ſucceſſion of lovers in one day—Fantome.
has driven out Tinſel, and I ſhall drive out Fantome.

Vel.

Vel. Ev'n as one wedge driveth out another—he, he, he ! you must pardon me for being jocular.

Sir Geo. Was there ever such a provoking blockhead ? but he means me well [*aside*] Well ! I must have satisfaction of this traitor Fantome ; and cannot take a more proper one, than by turning him out of my house, in a manner that shall throw shame upon him, and make him ridiculous as long as he lives———You must remember, Vellum, you have abundance of business upon your hands, and I have but just time to tell it you over ; all I require of you is dispatch, therefore hear me.

Vel. There is nothing more requisite in business than dispatch———

Sir Geo Then hear me.

Vel. It is indeed the life of business———

Sir Geo. Hear me then I say.

Vel. And as one has rightly observed, the benefit that attends it is four-fold. First ——

Sir Geo. There is no bearing this ! thou art agoing to describe dispatch, when thou should'st be practising it

Vel. But your ho-nour will not give me the hearing———

Sir Geo. Thou wilt not give me the hearing———

[*Angrily.*

Vel. I am still.

Sir Geo. In the first place, you are to lay my wig, hat, and sword ready for me in the closet; and one of my scarlet coats. You know how Abigal has described the ghost to you.

Vel It shall be done.

Sir Geo. Then you must remember, whilst I am laying this ghost, you are to prepare my wife for the reception of her real husband ; tell her the whole story, and do it with all the art you are master of that the surprize may not be too great for her.

Vel. It shall be done—but since her ho-nour has seen this apparition, she desires to see you once more, before you encounter it:

Sir Geo. I shall expect her impatiently. For now I can talk to her without being interrupted by that impertinent rogue Tinsel. I hope thou hast not told Abigal any thing of the secret.

Vel. Mrs Abigal is a woman ; there are many reasons why she should not be acquainted with it : I shall only mention six.——

Sir Geo. Hush, here she comes ! oh my heart !

Enter Lady *and* Abigal.

Sir Geo [*Aside, while* Vellum *talks in dumb show to the Lady.*] O that loved woman ! how I long to take her into my arms ! if I find I am still dear to her memory, it will be a return to life, indeed ! but I must take care of indulging this tenderness, and put on a behaviour more suitable to my present character.

[*Walks at a distance in a pensive posture, waving his wand.*

Lady. [*To* Vellum] This is surprising indeed ! so all the servants tell me : they say he knows every thing that has happen'd in the family.

Abig. [*aside.*] A parcel of credulous fools ! they first tell him their secrets, and then wonder how he comes to know them.

[*Exit.* Vellum, *exchanging fond looks with* Abigal.

Lady. Learned Sir, may I have some conversation with you, before you begin your ceremonies ?

Sir Geo. Speak ! but hold—first let me feel your pulse.

Lady. What can you learn from that ?

Sir Geo. I have already learned a secret from it, that will astonish you.

Lady. Pray what is it ?

Sir Geo. You will have a husband within this half hour.

Abig. [*aside.*] I am glad to hear that——he must mean Mr Fantome ; I begin to think there's a great deal of truth in his art.

Lady. Alas ! I fear you mean I shall see Sir George's apparition a second time.

Sir Geo. Have courage you shall see the apparition no more. The husband I mention shall be as much alive as I am.

Abig. Mr Fantome to be sure.   [*aside*

Lady. Imopssible ! I lov'd my first too well.

Sir Geo. You could not love the first better than you will love the second.

Abig.

Abig. [*aside.*] I'll be hang'd if my dear steward has not instructed him ; he means Mr Fantome to be sure ; the thousand pound is our own !

Lady. Alas ! you did not know Sir George.

Sir Geo. As well as I do myself——I saw him with you in the red damask room, when he first made love to you ; your mother left you together, under pretence of receiving a visit from Mrs Hawthorn, on her return from London.

Lady. This is astonishing !

Sir Geo. You were a great admirer of a single life for the first half hour; your refusals then grew still fainter and fainter. With what extafy did Sir George kiss your hand, when you told him you should always follow the advice of your Mamma !

Lady. Every circumstance to a tittle.

Sir Geo. Then Lady ! the wedding night ! I saw you in your white sattin night-gown ; you wou'd not come out of your dressing room, till Sir George took you out by force. He drew you gently by the hand——you struggled ——but he was too strong for you——you blushed, he——

Lady. Oh ! stop there ! go no further——he knows every thing.   [*aside.*

Abig. Truly, Mr Conjurer, I believe you have been a wag in your youth.

Sir Geo. Mrs Abigal, you know what your good word cost Sir George, a purse of broad pieces, Mrs Abigal——

Abig. The Devil's in him. [*aside.*] Pray Sir, since you have told so far, you should tell my Lady that I refused to take them.

Sir Geo. 'Tis true, child, he was forced to thrust them into your bosom.

Abig. This rogue will mention the thousand pounds, if I don't take care, [*aside.*] Pray, Sir, though you are a Conjurer, methinks you need not be a blab——

Lady. Sir, since I have now no reason to doubt of your art, I must befeech you to treat this apparition gently——it has the resemblance of my deceas'd husband ; if there be any, undiscover'd secret, any thing that troubles his rest, learn it of him.

Sir Geo. I must to that end be sincerely informed by

you, whether your heart be engaged to another; have you not received the addresses of many lovers since his death.

Lady. I have been obliged to receive more visits, than have been agreeable.

Sir Geo. Was not Tinsel welcome ?—I am afraid to hear an answer to my own question   [*aside.*

Lady. He was well recommended.

Sir Geo. Racks !

Lady. Of a good family.

Sir Geo. Tortures ?

Lady. Heir to a considerable estate.

Sir Geo. Death. [*aside*] And you still love him ?——I'm distracted !

Lady. No, I despise him. I found he had a design upon my fortune, was base, profligate, cowardly, and every thing that cou'd be expected from a man of the vilest principles——

Sir Geo. I am recover'd.   [*aside.*

Abig. Oh, Madam, had you seen how like a scoundrel he look'd when he left your Ladyship in a swoon. Where have you left my Lady ? says I. In an elbow chair, says he : and where are you going ? says I. To town, child, says he, for to tell thee truly, child, says he, I don't care for living under the same roof with the devil, says he.

Sir Geo. Well, Lady, I see nothing in all this that may hinder Sir George's spirit from being at rest.

Lady. If he knows any thing of what passes in my heart, he cannot but be satisfy'd of that fondness which I bear to his memory. My sorrow for him is always fresh when I think of him. He was the kindest, truest, tenderest—Tears will not let me go on——

Sir Geo. This quite o'erpowers me——I shall discover myself before my time. [*aside*]—Madam, you may now retire and leave me to myself.

Lady. Success attend you !

Abig. I wish Mr Fantome gets well off from this old Don——I know he'll be with him immediately.

[*Exeunt* Lady *and* Abigal.

          Sir George *solus.*

Sir Geo. My heart is now at ease, she is the same dear

woman I left her—now for my revenge upon Fantome—
I shall cut the ceremonies short—a few words will do his
business—now let me feat myself in form —a good easy
chair for a conjurer this !—now for a few mathematical
scratches—a good lucky scrawl, that—faith I think it
looks very astrological—these two or three magical pot-
hooks about it, make it a compleat conjurer's scheme.
[*Drum beats.*] Ha, ha, ha, Sir. are you there ? enter,
drummer.   Now I must pore upon my paper.

    Enter Fantome beating the drum.

  Sir Geo. Pry'thee don't make a noise, I'm busy.

                       [*Fantome beats.*

A pretty march ? pr'ythee beat that over again.

                [*He beats and advances.*

  Sir Geo. [*Rising*] Ha ! you're very perfect in the step
of a ghost.   You stalk it majestically. [*Fantome advances.*

  How the rogue stares ! he acts it to admiration ! I'll
be hang'd if he has not been practising this half hour in
Mrs Abigal's wardrobe.

    [*Fantome starts, and gives a rap upon his drum.*

  Pr'ythee don't play the fool !   [*Fantome beats.*

Nay, nay, enough of this, good Mr Fantome.

  Fant. [*aside*] Death ! I'm discovered.   This jade A-
bigal has betray'd me.

  Sir Geo. Mr Fantome, upon the word of an Astrolo-
ger, your thousand pound bribe will never gain my Lady
Trueman.

  Fant. 'Tis plain she has told him all.   [*aside.*

  Sir Geo. Let me advise you to make off as fast as you
can, or I plainly perceive by my art, Mr Ghost will have
his bones broke.

  Fant. [*to Sir George*] Look ye, old Gentleman, I
perceive you have learn'd this secret from Mrs Abigal.

  Sir Geo I have learnt it from my art.

  Fant. Thy art ! pr'ythee no more of that.   Look ye,
I know you are a cheat as much as I am.   And if thou
will keep my counsel, I'll give the ten broad pieces.——

  Sir Geo. I am not mercenary ! young man, I scorn thy
gold.

  Fant. I'll make them up twenty———

  Sir Geo. Avaunt ! and that quickly, or I'll raise such
    apparition, as shall ———

                             Fant

Fant. An apparition, old Gentleman ! you miſtake your man, I am not to be frighted with bugbears——

Sir Geo. Let me retire but for a few moments, and I will give thee ſuch a proof of my art————

Fant. Why, if thou haſt any *hocus pocus* tricks to play, why can'ſt not do them here ?

Sir Geo. The raiſing of a ſpirit requires certain ſecret myſteries to be performed, and words to be mutter'd in private————

Fant. Well, if I ſee through your trick, you will pro-miſe to be my friend !

Sir Geo. I will, attend and tremble.   [*Exit.*

Fantome ſolus.

Fant. A very ſolemn old aſs ! but I ſmoke him,——he has a mind to raiſe his price upon me. I could not think this ſlut would have uſed me thus——I begin to be hor-ribly tir'd of my drum. I wiſh I was well rid of it. How-ever I have got this by it, that it has driven off Tinſel for good and all ; I ſhan't have the mortification to ſee my miſtreſs carry'd off by ſuch a rival. Well whatever happens, I muſt ſtop this old fellow's mouth, I muſt not be ſparing in huſh-money. But here he comes.

Enter Sir George in his own habit.

Fant. Ha! what's that ! Sir George Trueman ! This can be no counterfeit. His dreſs ! his ſhape ! his face ! the very wound of which he dy'd ! nay, then 'tis time to decamp !   [*Runs off.*

Sir Geo Ha, ha, ha ! Fare you well, good Sir George. ————the enemy has left me maſter of the field: here are the marks of my victory. This drum will I hang up in my great hall as the trophy of the day.

Enter Abigal.

[*Sir George ſtands with his hand before his face in a muſing poſture.*

Abig. Yonder he is. O my conſcience he has driven off the conjurer. Mr Fantome, Mr Fantome ! I give you joy, I give you joy. What do you think of your thou-ſand pounds now ! Why does not the man ſpeak ?

[*Pulls him by the ſleeve.*

Sir Geo. Ha !   [*Taking his hand from his face.*

Abig. Oh ! 'tis my maſter !   [*ſhrieks.*

[*Running away, he catches her.*

F   Sir Geo.

Sir Geo. Good Mrs Abigal, not fo faft.

Abig. Are you alive, Sir ? ——He has given my fhoulder fuch a curfed tweak ! they muft be real fingers. I feel 'em I'm fure.

Sir Geo. What doft think ?

Abig. Think, Sir, think ? troth I don't know what to think. Pray, Sir, how——

Sir Geo. No queftions, good Abigal. Thy curiofity fhall be fatisfied in due time. Where's your Lady ?

Abig. Oh, I'm fo frighted—and fo glad !

Sir Geo. Where's your Lady, I afk you——

Abig. Marry I don't know where I am myfelf——I can't forbear weeping for joy——

Sir Geo. Your Lady, I fay your Lady ! I muft bring you to yourfelf with one pinch more——

Abig. Oh ! fhe has been talking a good while with the fteward

Sir Geo. Then he has open'd the whole ftory to her, I'm glad he has prepared her. Oh ! here fhe comes.

Enter Lady *follow'd by* Vellum.

Lady. Where is he ? let me fly into his arms ! my life ! my foul ! my husband !

Sir Geo. Oh ! let me catch thee to my heart, deareft of women.

Lady. Are you then ftill alive, and are you here ! I can fcarce believe my fenfes ! now am I happy indeed !

Sir Geo. My heart is too full to anfwer thee.

Lady How could you be fo cruel to defer giving me that joy which you know I muft receive from your prefence ? you have robb'd my life of fome hours of happinefs that ought to have been in it.

Sir Geo. It was to make our happinefs the more fincere and unmixt. There will be now no doubts to dafh it. What has been the affliction of our lives, has given a variety to them, and will hereafter fupply us with a thoufand materials to talk of.

Lady. I am now fatisfy'd that it is not in the power of ablence to leffen your love towards me.

Sir Geo. And I am fatisfy'd that it is not in the power of death to deftroy that love which makes me the happieft of men.

Lady.

Lady. Was ever woman so b'est! to find again the darling of her soul, when she thought him lost for ever! to enter into a kind of second marriage with the only man whom she was ever capable of loving!

Sir Geo. May it be as happy as our first, I desire no more! believe me, my dear, I want words to express those transports of joy and tenderness which are every moment rising in my heart whilst I speak to thee.

Enter Servants.

Butl. Just as the steward told us, lads! look you there, if he ben't with my Lady already.

Gard. He! he! he! what a joyful night will this be for Madam!

Coachm. As I was coming in at the gate, a strange gentleman whisk'd by me; but he took to his heels, and made way to the *George.* If I did not see master before, I should have sworn it had been his honour.

Gard. Hast given orders for the bells to be set a ringing?

Coachm. Never trouble thy head about that, 'tis done.

Sir Geo. [*to Lady*] My dear, I long as much to tell you my whole story, as you do to hear it. In the mean while I am to look upon this as my wedding day. I'll have nothing but the voice of mirth and feasting in my house. My poor neighbours and my servants shall rejoice with me. My hall shall be free to every one, and let my cellars be thrown open.

Butl. Ah! bless your honour, may you never die again!

Coachm. The same good man that ever he was.

Gard. Whurra!

Sir Geo. Vellum, thou hast done me much service today, I know thou lov'st Abigal, but she's disappointed in a fortune. I'll make it up to both of you. I'll give thee a thousand pound with her. It is not fit there shou'd be one sad heart in my house to-night.

Lady. What you do for Abigal, I know is meant as a compliment to me. This is a new instance of your love.

Abig. Mr Vellum, you are a well spoken man: pray do you thank my Master and my Lady.

Sir Geo.

Sir Geo. Vellum, I hope you are not difpleas'd with
the gift I make.

Vellum.

The gift is two-fold. I receive from you
The virtuous partner, and a portion too ;
For which, in humble wife, I thank the donors :
And fo we bid good night to both your ho-nours.

THE

THE
EPILOGUE.

Spoke by Mrs OLDFIELD.

TO-night the poet's advocate I stand,
   And he deserves the favour at my hand,
Who in my equipage their cause debating ;
Has plac'd two lovers, and a third in waiting ;
If both the first shou'd from their duty swerve,
There's one behind the wainscot in reserve.
In his next play, if I wou'd take this trouble,
He promis'd me to make the number double :
In troth 'twas spoke like an obliging creature,
For tho', 'tis simple, yet it shews good nature.

   My help thus ask'd, I cou'd not chuse but grant it,
And really I thought the play wou'd want it,
Void as it is of all the usual arts
To warm your fancies, and to steal your hearts :
No court-intrigue, no city cuckoldom,
No song, no dance, no music—but a drum—
No smutty thought in doubtful phrase exprest ;
And, Gentlemen, if so, pray where's the jest ?
When we wou'd raise your mirth, you hardly know
Whether in strictness you shou'd laugh or no.
But turn upon the Ladies in the pit,
And if they redden, you are sure 'tis wit.

   PROTECT him, then, ye fair ones ; for the fair
Of all conditions are his equal care.
He draws a widow, who, of blameless carriage,
True to her jointure, hates a second marriage ;
And to improve a virtuous wife's delights,
Out of one man contrives two wedding nights.
Nay, to oblige the sex in ev'ry state,
A nymph of five and forty finds her mate.

   Too long has marriage, in this tasteless age,
With ill-bred rallery supply'd the stage ;
No little scribler is of wit so bare,
But has his fling at the poor wedded pair.

                          Our

EPILOGUE.

Our author deals not in conceits fo ftale:
For fhou'd th' examples of his play prevail,
No man need blufh, tho' true to marriage vows,
Nor be a jeft tho' he fhou'd love his fpoufe.
Thus has he done you Britifh conforts right,
Whofe husbands, fhou'd they pry like mine to-night,
Wou'd never find you in your conduct flipping,
Tho' they turned conjurers to take you tripping.

F I N I S.